"*Nothing to worry about,*" Aunt Louise had assured. "Better that I rest, and I don't want you catching whatever bug I've come down with, Judy dear."

And then the shocking phone call came from her aunt's solicitor, Gene Reynolds. "Sorry to inform you, Miss Winters, but your aunt, Louise Jamison, has died."

Before Judy could catch a breath to respond, Reynolds continued in his monotone, "Looks like an apparent case of poisoning, according to initial reports."

Don't miss out on any of our great mysteries. Contact us at the following address for information on our newest releases and club information:

Heartsong Presents—MYSTERIES! Readers' Service
PO Box 721
Uhrichsville, OH 44683
Web site: www.heartsongmysteries.com

Or for faster action, call 1-740-922-7280.

The Gold Standard

Lisa J. Lickel

HEARTSONG
PRESENTS
MYSTERIES

For Mom and Dad

Acknowledgments:

Thank you to my early readers, Jill, Kyle, and my fellow
ACFW critters. Jessica Conant-Park's advice was invaluable,
and thank you to Victoria Merriweather who volunteered
to test drive. I'm grateful to Tammy Barley for her editing
skills, to Chief Jed Dolnick of Jackson, Wisconsin, for his
technical help, and to Larry Martin of Miller Funeral Home in
Kewaskum, Wisconsin, for his comments. Thank you to the
folks at Barbour Publishing for establishing a mystery lover's
book club. Let's have fun!

Matthew 6:21:
"For where your treasure is,
there your heart will be also."

ISBN 978-1-59789-525-5

Cover design: Kirk DouPonce, DogEared Design
Cover illustration: Jody Williams

*Our mission is to publish and distribute inspirational products offering
exceptional value and biblical encouragement to the masses.*

Printed in the U.S.A.

1

Judy Winters made divots in the lawn with her
church shoes, the ones with the high heels she saved
to wear once a week. She stopped her frenetic crisscross
pacing under the clothesline to look at her trail. Hah!
She could dethatch the entire yard if she kept walking.
She needed a few minutes away from everyone in the
house. Just a few minutes to grieve alone. And to think
about poison.

Hand at her brow to shield the sun's harsh light,
Judy surveyed her late aunt's farm. The half acre
surrounding the house sure could use work. What had
Aunt Louise done these past two years to allow her
once-lovely yard to decline into crabgrass and thistles?
Birds might enjoy the seeds, but she'd let the place
go. Only a recent lawn-mowing kept the dandelions
from taking over. Judy brushed a tear off her cheek,
wondering inanely who had mowed since Louise's
death.

Aunt Louise had reported feeling not up to par a
week ago, and Judy offered to come for a visit.

"Nothing to worry about," Aunt Louise had assured. "Better that I rest, and I don't want you catching whatever bug I've come down with, Judy dear."

And then the shocking phone call came from her
aunt's solicitor, Gene Reynolds. "Sorry to inform you,
Miss Winters, but your aunt, Louise Jamison, has
died."

Before Judy could catch a breath to respond, Reynolds continued in his monotone, "Looks like an apparent case of poisoning, according to initial reports."

What was the saying? That Louise bought the farm? Judy shook her head. What a horrible way to occupy her thoughts with her closest living relative freshly buried.

She continued to meander in the yard. Walking might keep her from wailing in grief in front of all these people. Louise had been all the family she had ever really known.

Gene Reynolds approached her as many of the guests were leaving. "Miss Winters, again our condolences." He took her hand into his pudgy moist one. Judy steeled herself not to shudder. "I have the legal paperwork regarding Louise's estate to go over with you at your convenience."

Reynolds's pupils flickered just enough for her to notice. *He has something to gain.* Sometimes her ability to decode body language came in handy. She'd picked up the skill in one of her continuing education courses and never seemed to be able to shake it.

Judy removed her hand from his. "Thank you." Other friends followed Reynolds to seek her out before taking their leave. She accepted a shoulder squeeze from a neighbor, an offering of sympathy, and an invitation to church while Reynolds stood guard on her right.

When they were alone, Judy asked, "Would this afternoon work for you, Mr. Reynolds? I don't want to rush or seem greedy, but I have two weeks left of the school year in Lewiston, and I need to get back to work."

"Miss Winters, this afternoon would be fine. How about I go to the office, pick up the files, and return . . .say, in an hour or so? We can go over everything here."

"Yes. I appreciate your time." She watched him clasp his hands together before joining his stately blond wife in the driveway. *He wants something, I can tell.*

"Good-bye." Judy waved at the last lingering guest, a woman dressed wildly in clashing plaids whose name she couldn't conjure. She could barely remember most of the names and faces of Aunt Louise's many friends.

If not for her boyfriend, Graham Montgomery, standing at her side all day until he had to leave for his own job, Judy didn't know how she would have dealt with her aunt's untimely and wholly unexpected death. Graham had not complained once about making small talk with strangers.

While she waited for Reynolds to come back, Judy continued to poke holes in the creeping charley under the clothesline. This was where they'd found Aunt Louise. No one had removed the laundry Louise carried to the yard after apparently ingesting some sort of lethal concoction. The basket still sat near the lilac bush, its clothing dried and no doubt hopelessly wrinkled. A yellow twin sheet that Louise had managed to pin up before her collapse snapped in the stiff breeze. At the resounding echo, she heard a flutter of cackles from the chicken coop, which was built against the barn a few hundred yards behind her. Louise kept animals on her working farm. Not just the noisy, colorful chickens, but cows, too. Judy visited on occasional weekends and even helped with chores under Louise's watchful eyes, but she'd grown up in Lewiston and didn't have the foggiest idea how to tend to their general day-to-day care.

Since she had rushed to tiny Robertsville from her home across Wisconsin in Lewiston upon learning the dreaded news of her former guardian's death, she had given little thought to the farm. Someone must have been caring for the animals. She hoped.

Poison. Louise's condition at the time of death led the emergency room doctor and the sheriff to suspect a toxic substance of some kind. She'd obviously been sick, and her skin was mottled. But Louise was the smartest person Judy knew. Her demise couldn't have been accidental, no matter what the doctor thought. Barry Hutchinson, the chief of police in Robertsville, agreed with Judy. But how to prove it? An autopsy report with a toxicology screen would not be available for weeks.

Judy resumed her agitated pace, shoving a bother-some wisp of brown hair behind her ear.

What was that in the laundry basket? Something moved. Judy peered more closely. There it was again. A black-tipped tail twitched from the depths of the willow carrier.

"Carranza! What are you doing in there?" Drat. She had forgotten about the ferocious cat Louise brought when she moved back home to the farm upon her own father's death two years ago. Carranza obeyed only Louise once he felt Judy abandoned him—and then only when it suited the feline. He lifted his head lazily in her direction and offered the malevolent stare she remembered well. She shivered. "Carranza, get away from there," Judy said again, weakly, hoping the animal wouldn't come her way. He raised his head, a bra strap entangled around his ear. Carranza shook his head and blinked then began insolently licking an outstretched paw, claws extended.

Enough of that. No way was she going to get into a power struggle with a pet cat. Her class of eighth graders, maybe; felines, no. Judy turned her back. The air was redolent with fresh-cut alfalfa. Her aunt rented acreage to a neighbor named Red Hobart. Judy inhaled enough to feel dizzy with the fragrance she normally loved. Today the scent nauseated her. She couldn't begin to imagine what Mr. Reynolds would tell her. Louise had never married or had children of her own and was the only child of her parents who'd both lived and died in Robertsville. Louise had spent her own adulthood raising a young, orphaned Judy. Maybe the property would be sold or something and she wouldn't have to worry about what to do. The farm had been in the family for generations, so she hoped there wasn't any major debt involved.

Heading toward the orchard, she almost tripped on an overturned bucket at the edge of the mowed area. Sinking to her knees to better see what was buried there, Judy pushed aside some of the foxtails to discover a tiny rose plant with buds so large they would have tipped the slender stalks had they not been held up by the sturdier weeds.

"Poor thing!" She yanked out some of the taller

field daisies that blocked the sunlight from the roses. "That should help a little." She should really try to tidy up the mess for the buyers and get the yard in shape. If only she'd known; really taken a good look at how much Louise had needed help, she would have . . . Would have what? Left her new job and come live with her aunt like some little girl who couldn't make it on her own? She was doing well, handling her independence. In fact, her principal had recently called her work "exemplary." Her students needed her.

Judy leaned back on her haunches, tilting her face to the sun, and listened. Catbirds in stereo with the tinny peaceful hum of distant cicadas took her mind off Lewiston and her job. She pushed herself to her feet to continue her inspection of the overgrown orchard. A flood of childhood memories from her many visits to the farm—apple blossom petals falling like snow and picking fruit in the fall—lulled her.

A cloud scuttered by overhead. Judy shivered. She rubbed her arms and checked her watch. Four thirty. Back in the main yard, she stopped in front of a gnarled stump. A single mossy branch dangled like a broken arm but bore a number of determined green leaves. Judy smiled and touched the deeply grooved brown bark. A bee buzzed nearby. She walked around to the other side where a weathered emblem appeared, carved into the trunk. Bending low, she traced a misshapen heart.

"Can I help you, Miss Winters?"

Judy looked up from her vulnerable crouch and froze at the sight of a well-built young man in aviator sunglasses striding up the unkempt lawn. The man came to a halt at the edge of her personal comfort zone. She watched lines form between his eyes and realized that her nervous smirk scored no points. Not a good way to make a first impression. Or second, since he knew her name.

"I don't think so," she said in her most polite voice. Judy pushed herself upward and held out her hand. "And you are?"

The man had his hands on his hips. He belatedly reached out to grab her hand. "Hart Wingate. Mine's the adjoining farm. I helped Louise and her father, when he was living, with chores. The police asked me to keep an eye out for strangers."

Judy nodded. "Yes. My aunt mentioned she'd had someone in to help her. I assumed she meant a hired hand. You don't know what really happened here, do you?"

"No. I wish I did. And I don't work for Louise. I helped her when she needed it after she came here when her father Harold died. I don't recall seeing you here before the funeral."

Taken aback, Judy opened her mouth to reply that she hadn't met him before, either, when they were hailed from the yard.

"Hello, there! So, you've met each other. Good." Gene Reynolds, accompanied by Red Hobart, who had changed to work coveralls from his funeral suit, stood waiting for her. "Red insisted on joining us, Judy. Says there's an important clause in the will that affects him."

"Hi, Red, Mr. Reynolds," Judy said. "So you both

know Mr., um, Mr.—"

"Wingate," Hart supplied.

"Sure, sure," Red said. "Hart's been great since even before Louise moved back home, mowing, taking care of the cows. Harold couldn't manage anymore, you know."

So Hart had mowed. And did chores. Aunt Louise's father had passed away so soon after her return to the farm.

Judy whirled around to face Hart. "Thank you for all of your help. Mr. Reynolds will advise me about what to do next and, I'm sure, contact you. Well, so long, then."

Reynolds kept quiet after Judy's little speech. She supposed she sounded rude, but this was Louise's farm, and that Wingate person said he had his own place next door. He must be busy enough with his own work without doing double duty.

Reynolds turned toward the house. "Shall we go, Judy?"

She followed Reynolds, Red close on their heels. The big old American gothic house seemed to leer at her. Without Louise, she felt like an intruder. Two years ago Judy had started her new job at Lincoln Middle School teaching eighth grade, and Louise said Judy was now grown and no longer needed her.

Louise, Louise, you're wrong. I need you now.

Judy was weary with decision making, meeting people she only vaguely remembered from her childhood when her aunt introduced her to neighbors. Tired of trying to find a place to put the food that arrived daily from her aunt's well-meaning friends. People who identified themselves as being from the state crime lab or the sheriff's department came twice before the funeral, asking permission to photograph and take samples from the barn, yard, and kitchen. As a teacher, Judy would have been curious about the work if she hadn't been overwhelmed by the reason for their presence.

Judy took a critical look around the kitchen while Reynolds tossed a scuffed leather briefcase onto one of four chrome chairs. He then rubbed his hands and indicated the room with a generous sweep of his right arm. "Vintage 1950s. People pay good money to get this look nowadays. What you have here is original."

She swiveled slowly. Reynolds found the light switch. An overhead chandelier garlanded with webs cast a hesitant forty-watt dent in the gloom. Judy noticed flies clustered in the corners of the shadowy high ceiling. *Why is it grunge is only noticed through a guest's eyes?* Cavernous cupboards overwhelmed a tiny window over the sink. Reynolds pulled out chairs, first for her and then for himself, and began to unpack his briefcase before sitting. Red Hobart hooked a seat of his own and straddled it backwards.

"Here we are," Reynolds announced, as if they'd all come from the four corners of the earth. "First, let me tell you that it has been a pleasure serving your family, and I hope that you and I will continue a long-term relationship. Louise was a truly honest, dedicated farmer and conservationist, greatly admired by all those in her circle. Upon her father's death we drew up a trust to try to prevent some of the unfortunate issues we encountered with his passing." Reynolds sorted through folders. He halted long enough to zero in on Judy with his black-framed plastic glasses. "Louise's father Harold passed intestate."

Judy gulped back a giggle at Reynolds's pronouncement and quirked an eyebrow in question.

"That means he never bothered to put his estate in order," the lawyer enunciated critically. "So let us begin."

A half hour later, Reynolds's raging torrent of handiwork slowed to a trickle. Judy was impressed with the amount of work that went into preserving the Jamison farmland. However, her aunt's last wish left her in consternation: Should Judy choose not to reside on and farm the property for at least three years, it would pass to KOWPIE, a local grassroots organization specializing in protection of natural areas. Louise's farm would serve as the district office.

"You've got to be kidding." Judy couldn't believe she'd heard correctly. "They call themselves 'cow pie'?"

Reynolds frowned behind the glasses. "I believe. . . ah, yes. Here. It stands for Keep Our Woods Pristine In Essence. But, of course, there are always ways to get around this little hiccup in your inheritance," Reynolds said. "Our office also handles real estate, you know, and I can tell you without reservation that I have a number of qualified offers on the table from nice people who are eager to make you comfortable. So comfortable that you need never worry about money again if you accept the appropriate deal."

He pulled a manila folder from his case. "I warned your aunt against those nut-job nature freaks. I've heard rumors about guns and bombs. They run some sort of military-style training camp to show how regular folks can create fortresses on their property. Make sure no honest, decent people can build a new home for themselves wherever they please. This is America! Anyone can build wherever he wants." He huffed. "Promising to care for the earth? The earth is here to take care of us, I say."

Judy stared at her entwined fingers on the speckled tabletop. "Do you know any of those people from KOWPIE? How did they get Aunt Louise to sign her property over to them like that? What if I decide I can't live here?"

"No, I don't know them. And I can't begin to understand how Louise would have dealt with such riffraff." Reynolds punctuated the word with a sharp grimace. Judy noticed something else about Reynolds's expression—a twitch of wiry black nose hair, gone in an instant. *He's lying. Why would he lie?*

She closed her eyes, recalling the sound of Louise's voice during a prior visit. "I practically had to call the police the last time. Those land-hungry grubbers drove right up my driveway and pounded on the door bold as brass. Man in a suit told me he wanted to buy just a little of my land. I'm sick and tired of those fools. Strangers. From Chicago. Imagine, anyone just waltzing around the neighborhood asking to buy other strangers' land. A person can't even expect privacy on his own property anymore."

Judy focused on the lawyer. "Thank you, Mr. Reynolds. I don't think my aunt wanted that."

Reynolds's little black pupils flickered with greater wattage than all the bulbs of the chandelier, and she felt certain Reynolds included himself as one of those nice people who would like the right to develop her farm into neat little subdivisions. Probably with a playground and a gas station and a dog park. Carranza would love that. "What about Mr. Hobart's claim?"

Hobart hadn't said a word during the whole presentation. She would have forgotten his presence if not for the emanation of machine grease and manure competing with alfalfa radiating from his person. Somehow, that smell made the kitchen feel more like home than Reynolds's musky cologne.

Red Hobart's family farm sprawled over two hundred acres across the country lane. Judy had heard the Hobart name mentioned by Louise and Harold for as long as she could remember. The Hobarts and Jamisons had lived and farmed together for generations.

"See, Miss Judy," Hobart began in his rural drawl, "the Hobarts did a favor for the Jamisons a long time ago. Long time. In exchange for this favor, the Jamisons promised the southwest forty to the Hobarts whenever this here farm passed from Jamison hands." Judy folded her arms and knew what was coming. She could almost hear the next line. Hobart's mouth formed the words as if he chewed on a long stem of grass. "You, ma'am, are not Jamison." He ducked his head to pinch an ant crawling up his bib then targeted her again in his sights. "No offense."

Judy was more offended by the "ma'am" than Hobart's accusation. She hated being "ma'am'd."

"Now, Red, strictly speaking, that's not true," Reynolds cut in. "Miss Winters, here, is a Jamison relation on her mother's side."

"So far back it don't matter none. Hardly more'n a drop of Jamison blood."

"Nevertheless, you are not entitled to that forty based on this clause, which says, and I quote, 'If said property passes out of the hands of any Jamison heirs or such heirs do not farm said property, the southwest quarter of the southwest quarter of section twenty-one shall be given to descendants of Clem Hobart to be used for his own purposes in gratitude for aid given during dangerous times.' End quote."

"Right. And I claim my promise now. If Missy Winters here ain't gonna farm, I got my rights to that forty."

Judy leaned forward, placing herself between the two men who'd subconsciously moved closer to each other during their exchange. "Please! Mr. Reynolds, Mr. Hobart. I haven't decided for sure yet, but I may stay here for the summer while I work on my master's degree. I want time to consider all the ramifications of my actions. Since I see that rental payment for the cropland covers the taxes and my needs are few, I should be able to take enough time to make a good decision. One that will benefit everyone involved."

Reynolds fixed Hobart with a glinty glare. "Judy may need to make some decisions soon regarding renters." He addressed her next. "If you recall what

I showed you earlier, Miss Winters, and take note of the due date, you'll see that the rent payments are in arrears. Have been for a while, as a matter of fact."

She understood him to mean that Red Hobart was the one who owed money. Hobart eyeballed Reynolds back.

Reynolds didn't give an inch. "Louise was too easy-going in those matters. We can talk more about that later."

Hobart blinked first. He took his leave with stiff formality, even tipping his John Deere cap in Judy's direction as she saw him out. When she returned to the table, Reynolds indicated three sets of keys. "Here are the keys the police put in my hands after the sheriff completed the initial investigation." Judy had used her own key when she first arrived and had not considered who closed up the outbuildings after Louise's body had been removed. "As you can see, these are marked for the house, these for the barn, and these, here—" Reynolds jiggled an old-fashioned ring with extra-large keys—"for the garage and car. Harold had a nice Monte Carlo that your aunt drove, I believe. Anyway, it's all yours now."

"Thank you," Judy said. Another thought occurred to her. "Mr. Reynolds?"

The balding man looked up and peered at her through his bifocals. He blinked. Judy was reminded of a picture of an owl in glasses.

"Yes?"

"Well, I wondered whether you knew if anyone else had any keys. Any of the neighbors?"

Reynolds cleared his throat. "That I wouldn't know." He looked back down at the papers in his hands. "I nearly forgot this last item. The stock report."

"Stocks?" Judy said. "I didn't know Aunt Louise owned any company stocks."

Mr. Reynolds looked at her over the top of the glasses. "Animals."

"Oh." Judy felt her cheeks warm. "Just before you came, out there in the orchard. . .that man—"

"Hart Wingate."

"Right. He said he'd been doing chores. Louise said she had some help, but I didn't pay attention at the time." Judy lowered her gaze to the chipped tabletop. "I assumed my aunt had a handyman or something. Mr. Wingate is renting Bryce Edwards's farm, isn't he?"

"That's right. I've been working with Country Properties LLC for some time, trying to encourage Edwards to sell now that he's moved into town."

Judy's shoulders sagged under the weight of the cumbersome details. She hadn't been given the luxury of being alone to vent the depth of her grief. She pulled in a breath and trudged on. "What's Country Properties?"

"Developers. Of course, any zoning change out here has to go through the town board. This farm is out of city jurisdiction, young lady. The board president, Slim Hobart, Red's cousin, and I don't always see eye to eye on coming changes. I strongly recommend you make a deal quickly. It's your land now. You don't have to listen to Hobart or the KOWPIE folks."

Or you? Judy eyed him. Reynolds began to

straighten out the papers on the table. "Just remember, this is one hot property."

Judy was more than ready to end the business-focused discussion about her inheritance. She wanted to look at the papers. Alone. "Thank You. Anyway, where do I sign, then, about taking over the title?"

"Right here, young lady." Reynolds pointed to the yellow stickers attached at the proper lines. "And here," he said as he shuffled more papers, watching her intently. "And here."

When Judy finished, she extended the stick pen. "Well, all right. Mr. Reynolds, I appreciate the house call and all. Um, when I leave, who should I call about taking care of the. . .stock?"

"Best to ask Wingate. He knows the place and has been doing it regular already." Reynolds stuffed papers into the worn calfskin case. He nodded down toward the Formica tabletop. "There's my card. Call me when you're ready to make a decision about selling."

Judy stood in the drive long after his taillights disappeared. Purple twilight gradually made shadows of the fence posts. A flock of sparrows settled on power lines across the road. A knot formed in her stomach. *I've never felt so alone.* At the sound of footsteps crunching in the gravel behind her, she tensed and spun around.

"Oh, you scared me," she said, recognizing her neighbor. Judy removed her hand from her thudding heart. "I apologize for sounding rude earlier. I really am grateful for all you've done to help us out."

"No need to apologize." Hart Wingate smiled. "If you need anything, don't hesitate to let me know."

"As a matter of fact, I wonder. . .if you have time, that is, would you consider continuing to do the chores while I'm gone? Or help me find someone I can hire? I have to go home for a couple of weeks for my job. But I think I'll come back."

"You're a teacher, right?"

Judy nodded. "Yes. School's out the first Friday in June."

They regarded the roosting birds for a quiet moment. "I'm happy to help. Louise and I worked together with the cattle. When you return I'd like to discuss our agreement with you. Louise was an interesting woman. We had some good conversations, and she taught me a lot about respecting our heritage." He smiled briefly again. "Even though your aunt managed to ruffle some feathers by her obsession with recycling, I'll miss her."

She couldn't recall anything about a cattle deal in the papers she'd just signed, but she was too exhausted to think about it now. Three years she'd need to give. Could she do that? What about her job? And what did Hart mean, Louise was obsessed with recycling? How could sorting one's aluminum and newspaper be considered obsessive? She and Louise naturally did that at home in Lewiston. Didn't anyone believe in recycling out in the country?

Judy looked at Hart through a blur of tears. "Aunt Louise gave up a lot to raise me. She barely got to spend any time back here before she died. Being cut down at fifty-four is no reward for the sacrifice she made on my behalf. It all happened so fast, I hardly know how to feel. All my aunt wanted was to come back here and live out a peaceful life. I need to know why she died. Maybe just to satisfy my own curiosity. Maybe so nothing like this—this murder of an innocent woman—ever happens to anyone else."

Hart seemed lost in thought. "I can't help you there. I'm angry about what happened to Louise, I admit, but I don't know what I can do to help."

Judy hugged her elbows tight. "That's all right. I shouldn't be bothering you about my personal business anyway. I'll check into your cow deal. Don't worry."

"Don't let me keep you from phoning your boyfriend or anything like that."

"I don't have a boyfriend," Judy heard the words tumble out of her mouth as though of their own volition. *What?* She blinked. Graham was her boyfriend, wasn't he? Why would she deny it? She cleared her throat. "At least, I've only been dating someone for a couple of months. Graham's been great. A shoulder for me to lean on when I need him."

"Apparently Louise didn't see it that way. I was here last week when that guy showed up. Louise ordered him to turn right around and leave."

2

I wouldn't do that if I were you," Graham crowed a warning at Jason. "Judy knows what you're thinking."

Judy glared at him over her hand of cards. "I do not!" Judy matched Graham's number of tiddledywinks in the pot.

Tonight, her last in Lewiston for the summer, Graham threw a little get-together for her farewell. Then he seemed strangely determined to wreck the experience. For all he'd avoided her for the last two weeks, she had been surprised that he'd gone to the trouble of a party. Graham, one of four general education specialists, worked in the school district as a regular substitute teacher in any classroom. He knew many more teachers than Judy did, for Lewiston boasted a good-sized district. At the gathering, he'd deliberately avoided her company and stocked mostly snacks and drinks he knew she didn't care for.

Jason Reed, Judy's eighth-grade counterpart at Lincoln, glanced speculatively across the table at both Graham and Judy. They played a friendly game of cards that involved no cash or even great skill to match numbers and suits for a high score. Winners received only a laugh and congratulations after each round.

"Fold." Jason lost his nerve and set his cards, facedown, in front of himself. "How do you do it?"

"It has something to do with the way she looks at you. Body language." Graham traded cards again.

Why would Graham dramatize her talent when he knew it irritated her? "A useful curse," Judy claimed now—and whenever anyone dared remark on her unusual ability to detect a hedge.

"Excuse me." Jason got up from the table. "No way can I beat a mind reader."

"Graham! Stop it!" Judy nudged him under the table. "Nobody will ever want to play cards with me again."

Graham grinned. "Do you give up?"

"Since we're the only ones left, yes!" She wanted to be fair. Graham meant well; he just liked to win.

"Does it work on women, too?" Rachel Burns, the sixth-grade intern asked. "Do me! Do me!" The woman sat eagerly in front of Judy and closed her puppy-brown eyes. "What am I thinking?"

"It doesn't work like that." In spite of her dismay, Judy laughed. "Rachel, open your eyes! I don't read minds."

"But Graham said—"

"I can't tell what anyone's thinking. Please don't make this into a big deal."

"Yeah," Graham said. "She can mostly tell when you're lying."

Rachel's eyes slid in his direction.

"Or when you've got a secret," Talia, Judy's next-door neighbor added.

And you've got a big one, Rachel, Judy thought. "Stop. Really. No one can read minds."

"Hah!" Jason came back to the table along with several others. "I remember now. Three weeks ago,

Bobby Carmichael was accused of hacking into your Web site and changing the results of your class survey. All the evidence made him innocent until you talked to him. How'd you get him to confess?"

Judy shrugged. "I don't really know. I just watch the way people, particularly teens, make extra little movements in their facial muscles. Or wriggle in their seats. Once in a while it clues me in on what they're really feeling. Come on, let's put on different music or something."

Her ability to interpret body language was becoming a big deal, though. . .one that Principal York relied on more and more to help straighten out disputes among the students. She hadn't even been aware of when she began to employ her little quirk in the classroom, but this past school year had been about the most peaceful she could recall once her students got the idea that there were few tricks they could pull on their teacher.

Judy watched Graham make a show of checking the ice in the cooler and restocking the beverages. His guests, mutual colleagues and friends of both or either of them, drifted into cliques to discuss their summer plans or rehash the recently finished school year. Graham wore sandals with beat-up khaki fatigue pants and a muscle shirt that showed his broad shoulders to advantage. He also sported one of his bean pod necklaces he'd brought back from somewhere. The kids loved to hear about how dangerous the pods were. Even rubbing them and licking your fingers could make a person sick. No one asked why Graham could wear them against his neck and not suffer ill effects. Many of the guests in the apartment admired his chummy, helpful personality and good looks. She couldn't decide if she felt a slight tinge of jealousy or simple unease about all she didn't know about him. Was he her boyfriend or not?

Graham opposed her desire to spend the summer alone in Robertsville at her aunt's—no, her—farm. He'd made that very clear the one time they spoke upon her return from the funeral. After that, no contact. At all. Judy wanted to be certain to make the right decision regarding letting the property go out of the family for the first time since the Jamisons settled in Wisconsin. Hart Wingate's talk of heritage caused her many sleepless nights. Her excuse of needing peace while she worked on her thesis research did not sit well with Graham. Maybe that was why he acted uncharacteristically cocky tonight.

Judy watched Graham, who was engaged in a lively conversation with Rachel, and Hart's explosive declaration the evening before she returned to Lewiston played in her mind. She had not tapped her reserve of bravado to bring up to Graham the subject of his alleged visits to Robertsville to see her aunt. The end of Hart's and her last conversation replayed itself at odd moments, like now.

"What are you talking about?" Judy had asked Hart.

"We're talking about the man who stood with you at the funeral, right? In the gray suit? Blond?" Hart asked. "He visited Louise at least twice, and I saw him downtown once. Strangers tend to stick out in a little town like this."

"You have to be mistaken. You talked to him?"

Hart had shaken his head. "The first time I saw him, he and Louise were out near the garage. I went into the barn to feed the calves, and by the time I was finished, he'd left. The other time, like I said, Louise was asking him to leave when I got there. I don't know if he even got out of his car. Little Chevy, a few years old, dark blue with a busted taillight. Just like he drove in the procession."

Judy believed that Hart told the truth. Tonight, after the talk about her unusual ability to read body language, she realized that she had not been able to read Hart's expression.

Why would Graham lie about going to Robertsville behind her back? No, that's not right. He just never told her he'd gone there. An omission of truth. Maybe he was avoiding her so he wouldn't have to tell her about his visits to Louise.

Eventually the guests trickled out the door, leaving her alone with Graham. He began to walk through his apartment, garbage bag in hand. Judy piled glasses in the suds-filled dish tub. Graham's short strides and taut set of shoulders would have clued anyone in to his emotions. When he told her to leave the dishes and go home so she wouldn't be tired for her drive tomorrow, she knew she couldn't begin an objective discussion regarding his clandestine visits to Louise. They were both tired and unhappy. Graham didn't appear ready to forgive her for "abandoning him for the summer," as he'd put it. And she felt equally cranky over Graham's lack of support.

Still, she didn't want to leave so disgruntled. She waited on the threshold. Graham stared over her shoulder. Judy's eyes settled on the large plant that grew to the ceiling. She touched the shiny, exotic, maroon-colored leaf. Where had she seen a plant like that before? "What's this plant called again?"

He shrugged. "Oh, something I picked up in southern California. I don't recall. I'll miss you so much. You have your cell?" He stepped around her to open the door.

"Graham, I want to talk to you soon about the farm, okay? I have some tough decisions to make."

Graham pulled her into his reassuring embrace and bussed the top of her head. "Okay, but not right now. I'm tired." He wore his most charming smile. "Everything will work out. Don't worry."

———

Once in Louise's house, Judy immediately recognized the strange plant in the dining room as a much smaller version of the one in Graham's apartment. The plant would make a good conversation starter, she decided. It had brilliant red flowers that reminded her of the magnified bacteria on slides she showed her students. She would tell Graham that since Louise kept the gift he'd given her, her aunt couldn't have harbored ill feelings toward him.

Judy stood at the refrigerator. She had cleaned out the overstuffed fridge before returning to Lewiston. Many of the well-meaning neighbors' dishes she'd been able to freeze, including a sponge cake that looked delicious. A few labeled containers were washed and stacked on the counter, waiting until they could be returned. Judy rummaged until she found a casserole and a cake, which she set out to thaw.

She walked through the house, exploring the area behind the kitchen. Aunt Louise had not done much to modernize the house when she moved back. Louise's parents, Harold and Una, had long ago added a tiny bathroom with just enough room to turn around in. The word *bathroom* was a misnomer for the sagging-floored room that contained a dark cubicle shower and rusty enamel sink. A toilet sporting a black seat hung lopsided from the wall behind it. Judy used it gingerly, afraid of ending up in the basement if the thing ever gave way. The single overhead light bulb turned on and off with a pull chain. Maybe a plumber in town could fix it up. If she sold, the new owners would want a decent bathroom. She checked her hair in the chipped and rusty mirror. Maybe she'd have her shoulder-length flyaway brown hair cut shorter for summer. She leaned forward to dab some moisturizer under her gray eyes. Faint smudges attested to her unrest at night. So much to think about with Louise's will, Graham, her future . . . Judy was used to hearing doors slam, a spike of steel guitar, and voices at her apartment complex. This strange silence, interrupted by the house creaking, kept her from sleeping all the way through until morning light.

Judy walked into another small room nestled behind the kitchen. A dark shadow hissed, and she shrieked.

"Carranza. How did you get in?" The fluffy cat

stretched regally on the daybed. He gave her a disdainful stare as if he owned the place and leapt down, stalking past her across the kitchen, tail straight out with twitching tip. Judy watched until he disappeared into the mudroom. Louise or someone must have put a pet door out there. She'd check later.

The room contained a tiny television her aunt had seldom watched. She folded a bright crocheted granny-square afghan, stopping to look through tall smudged windows out toward the long, low garage. Judy noticed a corner of the barn, and the barn reminded her about the animals. And Hart Wingate. She wondered how she could she get in touch with him or if she should just wait until she saw him in the yard.

A woman with long gray curls held back in a yellow-and-black-plaid headband pedaled a three-wheeled cycle into the yard. One of Louise's friends. Judy tried to jog the woman's name loose from her mind as she answered the charming clarion of the doorbell.

"My dear," the older woman greeted her. "I'm not interrupting you, am I? Have you just arrived?"

"Hello. No, you're certainly not interrupting. Did you ride all the way from town on that thing?" Judy ushered her caller into the dusty front parlor.

The woman nodded in satisfaction. "Three miles. Good exercise. Of course I don't go too fast anymore. . . ." The guest prattled all the way into the kitchen and throughout the time it took Judy to pour lemonade for them.

"I want to tell you how sorry I am about Louise. I heard it was poison. What a way to go. I might have suspected something like that, though. Louise could never have died of old age or anything so mundane. All those mysterious callers. Oh! Dear, you forgot to add the sugar."

"I did? I'm so sorry." Mysterious callers? Poison? What in the world? Judy went to look for some in the cupboard while she tried to frame a question.

"To the right, dear. By the sink. That's right," the woman guided her.

"Callers? You said mysterious people visited Aunt Louise?" Judy said when she brought the sugar bowl back to the table.

"Don't say I didn't warn her." The woman spooned a large helping of sugar from the bowl and stirred.

"Um, Mrs.—"

"Oh! My manners. Of course you wouldn't remember me. How silly. You didn't visit very often, and why should Louise bring a bright thing like you to visit an old woman? Saw you in church, though. Good girl. I was really a friend of Louise's father, you know. My name's Ardyth. Ardyth Belters."

"Mrs. Belters—"

"You can call me Ardyth." She patted Judy's hand. "I know you can be respectful to your elders, being a teacher and all." Ardyth sniffed. "The young ones, now. They have no respect." She sipped and held her glass in Judy's direction. "You teach them to do the right thing. I know you will, pretty thing like you."

"Thank you. But you were saying? About Louise's visitors?"

"Well, I'm of the opinion they wanted the farm

only for their shooting and what all. Environment schmironment." Ardyth watched her reaction over the rim of the glass.

Judy tried to take in Ardyth's expression. Was the woman crazy? Ardyth's expressive eyes remained guileless. *If she believes what she's telling me, then what?*

"What did the police say about your theory?" Judy asked.

"Hah! County people. Useless. Busy. Barry knows what I'm talking about. If we want anything done, we have to keep him on our side."

Judy noted the "we." Ardyth's pupils pulsed slightly. She was sincere. "You mean Barry Hutchinson, the chief of police?"

Ardyth bobbed her curls. "I know this farm's out of his jurisdiction, but he knows the score. For a young fella."

Chief Hutchinson had a grown son, Judy knew.

"He knows about those KOWPIE folks. KOWPIE, indeed. Bunch of fools with guns. I also came to tell you to watch for Bryan, my grandson."

"Oh?"

"Louise had the idea to have him help search for the treasure. He's been enthusiastic with that detector thing that young Hart Wingate owns."

Judy stopped mid-drink and stared at Ardyth. Asking about poison drained away. "Did you say *treasure*?"

Ardyth looked at her with bird-bright eyes. "That's right. Surely Louise told you?"

3

I don't recall hearing anything like that," Judy said faintly. "Tell me what you know."

"Come to the parlor," Ardyth said. She rose and scurried through the dining room and a set of glass parlor doors leading to the front room. Judy followed.

"Here." Ardyth found what she sought and held out a photograph for her to see.

"That's us—your uncle Harold and me and Bryce Edwards. I don't suppose you'd recognize Bryce. This photograph goes *way* back to when we were in school together."

Three curly-headed children dressed alike in overalls hung onto a huge tire swing. Judy could see Harold's barn in the background.

Ardyth smiled, showing a dimple by the side of her mouth. "That old tree isn't even there anymore. Hit by lightning during one terrible storm." She paused. "Why, I believe that was the year before Harold and Bryce went off to find their fortunes."

"You mean when they caught the gold bug?" Judy asked.

"That's right. Old Joe Borden had been to Alaska and back, filling the boys' heads with tales of gold just glimmering in streams." She waved her hand and sighed. "Harold brought himself back a bride."

"Aunt Una," Judy supplied.

"Right. And Bryce. . .he came back alone, nothing

to show for his foolishness." Ardyth's mouth buttoned. She sniffed. "Well, I guess I shouldn't say 'nothing.' To make a long story short, he *claimed* he had a great treasure. Never showed anyone, though. Then, long after I moved to St. Louis and had my own family, he claimed he lost it out here somewhere. Such foolishness. Carelessness. I, for one, didn't believe he had any gold in the first place. He just didn't care about things like he used to. Anyway, I had to look after my own interests, my own family." Her smiled faded.

Judy had the impression this version of the story was far from complete.

"So now you're the keeper of the farm and its secrets," Ardyth continued. "What are your plans—a pretty girl like you? You're not married, I know. Where's your boyfriend? That good-looking young man from the funeral?"

Ardyth's rapid-fire questions made her head spin. Judy pulled in a breath and decided to answer the first one. "I don't really know what to do. I don't know anything about farming. I just want to stay here for a few weeks to try to make the best decision. I know I need to find out more about that environmental group. And Graham is back home in Lewiston."

"What you may not know is that I think Louise started to change her mind once she found out what those folks really wanted." Ardyth dropped this new bomb casually. She set the photograph back down on the lamp table, making the beads on the lampshade quiver.

Judy felt as if she were lost in some weird maze.

"What made you think that?" She led the way back to the kitchen, past the strange plant Louise had in a corner of the dining room.

Ardyth rubbed at gathering dust on the shiny lobed leaves and poked at the bristly red flowers. "Is this new? I don't remember seeing a plant like this in here before. I think this could use a drink, dear." She never paused to hear an answer to her question but walked on and pointed to the pots of African violets on the sideboard. "Check those, too, won't you? We all just figured Louise would sell out to Country Properties. No heir, you know. You were all she had, and she wanted to leave you something."

"Country Properties?"

"The Reynolds couple." Ardyth sniffed again. She leaned against the counter near the sink and rinsed her glass.

Judy tried a different tack. "How could Bryce have lost something on this farm instead of his own property? And didn't he ever say what the treasure was?"

"Why, of course! Gold, dear. The gold he panned for in Alaska when he and Harold went out there fresh from high school. Somehow, years later, he involved Louise," Ardyth said. "Way back when your aunt was just a little girl. Seems mighty strange to me that no one's gotten any dander up looking for that nonsense until we thought she planned to sell the place. Bryce goes in and out of town on business all the time. You never know where he is. Someone must believe the treasure is here."

"Ardyth, you don't believe the treasure had anything

to do with Aunt Louise's death, do you?"

Ardyth patted her hand. "Now, dear, don't get yourself all in a tizzy. Chief Barry will take care of everything. He's got the hospital lab doing double duty and the state folks all worked up to find the poison. He'll figure everything out."

The older woman began to gather her scarf and purse when she stepped back from the table.

"Ah, Carranza," Ardyth said in her cozy conversational style. "Thank you, but I have to tell you, Cat just isn't interested in your treats."

Judy closed her eyes and put her hand on the back of a chair at the sight of the ragged gray feline. Carranza sat, meek as you please, in front of Ardyth's chair, a paw on the body of a quivering brown rodent.

Ardyth met Judy's shock with a twinkle in her eyes. "Carranza has been attempting to court my Cat since they first met. He often brings an offering. I see he's had to go outside to get a deer mouse, which means he's doing a good job of keeping the house clear for you." When she bent down to put a hand on Carranza's head, Judy's intake was audible.

"Don't you worry," Ardyth assured in a rumbly, affectionate tone. "I'll bring Cat out again soon, I promise. You should take this mousy out of here now, though."

Judy blinked at the sight of Carranza picking up the mouse and trotting into the mudroom. She gulped another surprised breath at Ardyth's adept handling of Carranza.

"If you can, don't rush into selling just yet." Ardyth

resumed her no-nonsense voice.

Judy refrained from commenting on the cats and tackled the issue of the property. "I have the summer to think it over." She turned toward the counter. "Would you like something to eat?"

Ardyth refused her offer of lunch. "I'll be in touch. And don't you hesitate to call if you need anything at all."

Perhaps Ardyth's offer included helping with Louise's cat. Judy began to formulate a plan which involved the removal of Carranza to join Cat.

After Ardyth pedaled off, Judy went to investigate the garage. A shushing, sifting noise came from the barn, and she changed direction. The sound had an irregular rhythm, like waves washing onto a beach. Judy reached the half-door entrance and stopped to catch her breath. A man's voice drifted out to her.

"Hey, Bucky, there now. Don't be so greedy. This'll—" The voice cut off and changed tone. "Who's out there?"

Judy recognized the voice of Hart Wingate and called into the barn. "It's me, Mr. Wingate. Judy Winters."

The rhythmic noise began again. After a moment, Hart called out. "Well, are you coming in? Or are you just going to stand there? And latch the door behind you."

Judy felt around at the door handle. After an anxious moment she reached her hand over the door and tried to unlatch it from the inside. She poked at the handle uselessly until the catch lifted. Somehow she hated to bother Hart for help just to open a silly door.

When she finally got inside and reset the handle, she halted at the sight of her handsome neighbor.

"Lock looks easier than it is," Hart drawled.

Judy gave her hair a pat. "First time's a doozie," she said. "But I think I got the hang of how the latch works now." She stepped past him along the cement aisle. Three fluffy gray-and-black-striped tabby cats trotted in her direction along a floor strewn with straw, and hopefully, just mud. She turned, examining the room. Her gaze wandered up the long cement causeway. Hart was pouring some kind of grain from a large feed bag into a pen that held three scrawny reddish-brown spotted calves with white faces. Red had told her the cows were being taken care of, and she hadn't questioned him. Too many other things had claimed her attention since she'd arrived for her to worry about such details.

The calves shuffled and nosed each other, bleating, for a better place at the front of their enclosure.

"I read the stock report," she told Hart.

"Good." He didn't even break the rhythm of filling buckets.

"They sound like goats."

"They're hungry," he said.

She had a hard time looking away from the picture Hart made, standing there under the swaying, bare lightbulb, dressed in jeans with work boots, a blue T-shirt, and heavy gloves. She couldn't help compare him to Graham. Graham was bulkier and stood roughly a handbreadth taller than Hart. Graham had short blond hair compared to Hart's sun-streaked brown locks. Hart continued his chore wordlessly until Judy became uncomfortable. She coughed and reached to pet one of the cats that wound around and between her ankles.

"About our agreement, then," Hart began without preamble when he closed up the feed bag. He met her eyes briefly. "Louise bought the original animals and kept them here, but I get the offspring in exchange for providing the feed and taking care of them." He gestured at the calves. "These are the first three of the cattle that belong to me."

"What kind are they?"

"Herefords. Beef cattle. There's no money in milking nowadays, and I can't afford the equipment anyway. Angus would be better, but they're more expensive."

Judy nodded, though she had no firsthand knowledge of raising cows, but she could learn. Angus sounded Scottish. She'd look it up. One of the calves raised a tail, and Judy wrinkled her nose.

"Thank you for taking care of the animals. I—I'd like to learn about caring for them. I can take over the chores and, um, running the farm. If Louise did it, I should be able to."

Hart's whole face changed to show incredulity when he raised both eyebrows. He pulled sunglasses from a front pocket, stuck them on his nose, and moved past her out of the barn, shaking his head.

Judy didn't need any of her reading-faces tricks to know she'd offended him. "Wait. Please. I didn't mean to say that. Taking care of animals is hard. I'm sure you work hard."

She debated between following Hart out the door and whether to turn off the light. She decided the light could wait then fumbled for a few bothersome moments with the finicky latch on the barn door. By the time she hurried into the yard, Hart was nowhere to be seen.

"And Aunt Louise wondered why I'm not married," Judy said to herself, "with my winning ways and all."

She started around the side of the barn and stopped short at the sight of empty acres before her. Even she knew that something should be growing by now if crops had been planted. Red Hobart signed the rental contract, but as Gene Reynolds had indicated, he was far behind in payment. Maybe he didn't have enough cash to even buy seed. Only the short acreage in front of the barn had been cut, hence the alfalfa scent. Had Red or Hart done the work? She looked back at the barn, neat with white trim, fences sporting new crosspieces here and there, and others well-mended. The sound of an engine starting up reminded her that she'd been following Hart to apologize for saying something hurtful. She didn't even know how to turn on a tractor, much less where to drive. A tractor with a bucket lift full of hay bales rumbled into view. Hart roared off toward another enclosure, dirt swirling high in the air after escaping from underneath the gigantic black tires.

Judy climbed the fence and began to follow him, heedless of where she walked, until she felt her foot sink into something soft. She closed her eyes. An acrid aroma stung her nostrils. She was tempted to stomp her foot in frustration, but of course that would only make the situation worse. Instead, she gingerly lifted her shoe-clad foot, which was now encased up to the instep with fresh manure. She turned and headed back to the house.

As she opened the back door, she could hear the cows shifting and plodding and mooing in the distance, intermingled with the sputter of the tractor. What was she doing on a farm? She wasn't cut out for this. Judy left the offending shoe outside and walked through the large pantry off the kitchen, which Louise used as a mudroom.

The doorbell announced a visitor. Judy shook her head. What a day already. "I'm coming!" she shouted through the hall. She opened the door to a distinguished-looking gentleman holding a soft golfer's cap. He smiled and held out one hand to her then stopped midway, looking down at her feet. The smile turned into a chuckle.

"I'm sorry. I must have caught you in the middle of something."

Judy's puzzlement turned into chagrin as she realized she was wearing only one shoe.

"Oh, my. Well, it's just one of those. . .things. Hello." Judy tried to cover her embarrassment by wiping her hands on the striped dish towel she'd picked up on the way. She stepped back into the hall.

"I think I remember you. Mr. Edwards, right?"

"That's right. You have a good memory, young lady. Bryce Edwards. I'm sorry about little Louise. I've been out of town right up until an hour ago."

"Yes, thank you." Judy didn't mention that he'd been the subject of a recent discussion with Ardyth

Belters. "You're kind to come so quickly. Won't you come in? I think there's still some coffee."

"Thank you. Don't mind if I do."

Bryce Edwards, Uncle Harold's lifelong friend and former neighbor, followed her back to the kitchen.

"Folks have been so kind," Judy said. "Cake?"

"Certainly. I recognize Ruth Harris's golden sponge, if I'm not mistaken. That coffee sure smells wonderful."

Judy began to search through the cupboards only to find Bryce opening one for her on the other side of the sink, where a variety of mugs hung from hooks.

"May I help myself?" Bryce asked.

"Oh! Of course. I haven't had much chance to memorize the cupboards. Aunt Louise must have rearranged things since the last time I visited."

"And a fresh cup for you?" he inquired gently. "How do you take yours?"

"Just black." Judy sat at the table.

"It's been a long day for you, I see," Bryce commented, setting filled cups in front of them. "I stopped by the cemetery on the way here. Louise will be at peace next to her parents."

"Did you hear about how she died?" Judy bit her bottom lip. Each time she spoke of the loss of the aunt, the woman who'd sacrificed her own happiness to raise her, a fresh wave of grief hit.

Bryce sat across from her. "The news has gotten around. I had a call from a mutual friend while I was down at the home office. I hope there's some mistake. Louise was too careful to accidentally get into poison."

"That's what I think, too." Judy sipped the coffee, more to hide her quivering lips than to add caffeine to her agitated state. "Between watching strangers in uniforms trample all over the yard and barn, burying my closest living relative, and trying to figure out what to do with the place, I'm just lost."

Her visitor nodded in sympathy. "I saw Hart's truck. He'll take care of the chores as long as you need him."

Judy gnawed at her lip. "Yes. We spoke a little while ago in the barn."

Bryce gave her a friendly inspection. "Little Judy, all grown up. Harold was so proud of you, you know. Could have bust when he heard you were attending college, wanting to be a teacher. Too bad he didn't live to see you graduate. And Louise. Can't believe she's gone, too." He contemplated the coffee mug with a blank stare and a down-turned mouth before he took a sip.

Judy warmed her hands on her cup. "So what are you doing these days, Mr. Edwards?"

"Call me Bryce. Oh, I still work at consulting for the farm implement group. That's where I was when poor Louise passed. . .in St. Louis at the home office. I gave up farming, you know, many years ago, to follow my love of engineering. About the time poor Una passed on, I guess. Now I rent out the land and the house to young Hart Wingate since I moved into town. Hart—he's a good man. Godly, too. He ushers in our church, him so young and all. Goes to show he's a blessing to have around, I can tell you, because the regular church team made a place for him. They're sticklers about who they allow into their posse."

"So Mr. Wingate's a local, then?"

"No. We met at a seminar. He'd started graduate school but had to find something different for a spell. He said he was looking for a change and decided to move down here. His family's from Goodwin, up north, where they have a large dairy operation. Hart's a tagalong. You know, a whaddya call it? A later-born child. His siblings are a good decade older."

"Oh." Judy doubted Hart would appreciate Bryce's biographical sketch. So she and Hart had something in common: few close relatives of the same age. "Well, anyway, how have you been? And your family?"

Judy could have kicked herself. She'd forgotten that Bryce had never married.

"Oh, my sister and hers are just fine, thanks," Bryce replied, with no hint of awkwardness. "That's right, you and Annie used to play together, didn't you? My sister's youngest, that is. She's married now, two kids. Lives over in Port Williams. Maybe you could give her a call. How long are you planning to stick around?"

"I have to think about my schedule. School's out for the summer, so work isn't an issue, but I'm working on my master's degree."

Judy looked at the lines in Bryce's face, his gentle pewter eyes full of sympathy.

"I want to make sure things are wrapped up here." She took another drink of her cooling coffee and picked up the deed from the table. "If I do stay here for the summer, I want to have a decent bathroom. Do you know anyone who might have time for a remodeling job? I'm giving short notice, I know."

Bryce put up a hand to stroke his chin. "I did hear before I left that Mrs. Shipley died." He held the hand out, palm toward her. "Now, I don't have a morbid streak. Mrs. Shipley was old and full of years, as they say. She simply had more money than she knew what to do with and had Clyde working on her place again. I bring this up in light of the fact that Clyde may now have an opening."

"Clyde?"

"That would be Clyde Greves, a local handyman. People wait for months for him when they have a project. Let me give him a call for you right now. How would that be?"

"Great. Thank you." Although she'd promised herself earlier not to rush in to any decisions, making the one bathroom of the house more comfortable could only help in the long run. The amount of money Louise had in her account would be adequate for a project like this. She listened to Bryce's end of the conversation.

"Thank you, Roxanne. Yes, that's right. Poor Louise. You're right; she was a lovely person, even if she did have a way of making a body feel guilty on occasion. Right. Too much trash. Yes. Judy's here now. She's thinking of staying. . . . No, just the summer right now. That's right, she's a schoolteacher. What's that? Well, I'll let her know. Now, what we really want to know is if Clyde could come by and do some work on the place." Bryce nodded. "Sure, sure. You have him call Judy Winters. Okay. Good-bye now."

He returned to the table and confirmed that Clyde would call her later to schedule an appointment. "Roxanne seemed to think he would want to fit you in."

"That's wonderful. And you know him pretty well? He's trustworthy?"

"I've never had him do any work for me, but I can give you the number of someone else to act as a reference."

"I don't want to seem suspicious, but I'm new here and I need to be careful."

"No, no, you have good sense, Judy. Louise taught you well. Clyde's wife Roxanne wanted me to tell you she heard there was going to be an opening for a teacher at the elementary school."

"Oh. Well, I already have a job I like. That's awfully kind of her, when she doesn't even know me."

"Your reputation precedes you. Anyway, the Jamisons are an old family, well thought of around here. And you're one of them."

Judy tingled at the compliment. At least not everyone felt the same way as Red Hobart. "Ardyth told me the strangest tale today."

The lines around Bryce's eyes crinkled. "Let me guess. Something to do with missing treasure."

"That's right." A rap on the screen door interrupted her. "Excuse me. I'll just see who that is."

Judy went to the door and found Hart standing on the porch.

"Hi." Judy put her hand on the screen door.

Hart's smile showed a suspicious sparkle, and her lips turned up in automatic response, until the dip of

Hart's eyes toward the back step reminded her of what she'd left there. Judy twitched her nose. "Yes?"

"Hi," Hart said. "I just wanted you to know that I finished in the barn. Did you want me to take care of the chickens?"

Judy glanced down at her hand on the door. "Thanks, Mr. Wingate. I'm—"

"Hart."

Carranza appeared at his feet, stood on hind legs, and put a paw on Hart's knee. Judy watched, open-mouthed, as Hart bent to pick him up. The animal eyed her with unfathomed emerald orbs then rubbed his ears against Hart's chest and uttered an intermittent growling purr.

Judy realized she was staring, swallowed, and flushed. "I'm really sorry about sounding as if taking care of a farm is child's play."

"That's all right, ma'am. I know you don't have much experience at this sorta thing. I was guilty of acting in haste myself. No harm done."

Again, she couldn't determine if her neighbor was truly sorry or being sarcastic. She decided to take the apology at face value. "Tell you what—call me Judy. I'm not old enough to be ma'am'd."

The lines around Hart's eyes crinkled, showing the tan of spending a lot of time outdoors in all weather. "Agreed."

"Carranza likes you, I see. That's some high praise."

Hart grinned. "Sure. This fella is a great mouser. A big help in the barn, aren't you, buddy?"

Carranza yawned hugely, baring his fangs. Judy

turned her head toward the kitchen where she could hear Bryce shifting in his chair.

"Isn't that Bryce's car?"

"Yes, he just got back and stopped in to offer his condolences." With another glance into the kitchen she said to Hart, "I really do want to learn as much as I can about the place. Will you teach me?"

Hart tilted his head while he returned her gaze. "Yes, sure thing."

"Thank you. Maybe we can start next week? I'm sure you're busy with your own place. Please don't let me keep you."

"Sure. I'll just be on my way. In the next couple of days, I'd like to drop off a copy of the agreement Louise and I had regarding the cattle, if I may." Carranza leaped from his arms and disappeared around the side of the house as if knowing the conversation was over.

"Of course. I'll be gone this weekend, but I'll look over the papers when I get back. Thank you."

"Just call if you have any concerns before then. See you around."

After she closed the door, she realized she'd forgotten to ask how to reach him. She smacked her forehead as she walked into the kitchen.

"Was that Hart?" Bryce asked.

"Yes. He said he finished tending to the cattle. I feel so stupid about everything around here." Judy plunked herself down at the table. Bryce leaned over and patted her hand, much like Ardyth had.

"Now you just wait and sleep on that feeling, Judy." Bryce winked. "Things always seem better when you've had a chance to think about them. I have some business with young Hart. I'd best see if I can catch him. Thank you for the coffee. I'll be in touch." He grabbed his cap and strode out the back door.

Judy set the oven on low to heat up the casserole she'd set out earlier. While she explored the cupboards, her thoughts turned to home and Graham. Talking to Graham about his visits to Robertsville and the treasure would have to wait for another day.

The treasure! How on earth did she let Bryce get away without answering her question? Could someone have thought this treasure was worth taking a person's life? But more importantly, what kind of person would resort to such drastic measures? Judy shivered. She'd be alone in this big farmhouse much of the time. She dug her cell phone out of her handbag and vowed to carry the thing with her at all times.

While she ate her solitary supper, her mind raced. Red Hobart wanted land. Why did Ardyth seem so concerned about Judy selling? And why didn't Bryce seem more concerned about his lost treasure, whatever the treasure might be? Just who was behind KOWPIE? Had someone from that organization found out about Aunt Louise wanting to change her will and killed her before she had the chance?

Robertsville folks seemed nice. Maybe a little too nice if strangers wanted her to stay so badly they'd offer to fix her house immediately and tell her about a job opportunity.

Judy put thoughts of the handsome, helpful, cat-loving neighbor on the back burner.

4

The next few days crawled by as Judy began to set the neglected house to rights. She began with a thorough cleaning of the main rooms downstairs and started to open the upstairs windows for an airing. Evening sounds of cattle shuffling, distant coyotes, and even Carranza's comings and goings soon felt natural.

Nearly a week had passed since she'd seen Graham. Judy tossed the dust rag on the counter. Graham had not tried to call her, so she'd give him a buzz.

Judy perched on the steps of the wide front porch as she dialed and mulled over what she wanted to say. Once she heard his voice, loneliness engulfed her. In an effort to keep him talking, she hesitated to ask about his alleged visits to Louise and instead encouraged his lengthy discourse on the goings-on in Lewiston.

"So, isn't there any way I can change your mind about coming home, babe?" Graham asked.

Judy winced. "Graham. . .I don't like you calling me 'babe,' " she said. His throaty chuckle and apology made her long to be in his presence despite her pet peeve. "Actually, I'm coming back to check on things this weekend."

"When can I come visit you there?"

"I know you're busy," Judy said, unsure why the thought of meeting Graham at the farm bothered her. Ardyth's reminder that she was alone popped into her head. She rose, restlessly pacing and searching the yard . . .for what?

"So how about it?" Graham asked again.

"I have something to ask you," Judy said, dodging his question. "Let's talk on Saturday at your place before your shift at the club."

"Give me a hint," he pleaded.

"We'll both have something to think about this week. Bye, Graham."

Judy severed the connection and slipped the phone into her pocket. After collecting the mail, she decided to go into Robertsville. She could ask at the Reynoldses' office about transferring some money and paying the utility bills. Then she could supplement the dwindling frozen leftovers with fresh food from Carl's Market.

Invited into the inner office at Reynolds's suite, Judy looked around at the pleasantly decorated room as she took her seat. Dominated by a huge glass-topped desk littered with several manila files and piles of papers, she stared at the foreign sight of a manual typewriter anchoring one side of the workspace with antique regality.

"So you've decided already? That's good." Reynolds opened a file he removed from a basket on his left.

"Well, no." Judy shifted in the fake leather chair across from him. "Or maybe. If you're asking did I decide to follow my aunt's will, the answer is 'not yet.' I plan to stay here for the next several weeks." She leaned forward. "I am having the bathroom remodeled, however. Bryce Edwards recommended Clyde Greves."

Reynolds folded his hands and fixed her with a puzzled stare. "Greves. Yes, we know him. Edwards told you about him, you said?"

"Yes. Is there a problem?"

"No, no. I seem to recall. . ." Reynolds leaned over and pressed the intercom button. "Laura."

Upon her acknowledgement, Reynolds asked, "Don't we have a file or something on the Greveses? Something about arrest for civil disobedience?"

At Judy's gasp, Reynolds smiled slightly.

"I'll check. Give me a couple of minutes," his wife replied.

Reynolds depressed the button and resumed his hands-folded mock serene position at his desk. Judy bit her lower lip. "Mr. Reynolds, I haven't engaged him yet."

Reynolds held his hand up for silence. Laura brought in a folder. "Hello, Miss Winters. I heard you planned to stay at the farm for a while."

"Yes, that's right." How had Laura Reynolds heard Judy's news while her husband Gene had not? Judy's gaze slid to the intercom.

"You be sure and give us a jingle if there's anything we can do for you." The woman returned to her own desk but left the adjoining door open.

Meanwhile, Reynolds located the information. "See, here." He slid a yellowed newspaper article across the expanse of his desk.

Judy studied the clipping for a moment about a group that had protested removal of old growth timber in the Great North Woods before observing Reynolds's twitching right cheek muscle. "The article is from 1978."

"Yes, but once a criminal. . ." Reynolds pushed his heavy glasses up the bridge of his nose and whispered,

"You just can't tell with those types. Miss Winters, I'd advise you to find someone else."

"Thank you, Mr. Reynolds. I appreciate that. But now I'd like to know more about the bank accounts and how to pay bills, please."

Reynolds confirmed with a phone call to the bank that they merely waited on her signature to change the account information. He also informed her that the deed transfer to her name should be finalized soon.

"Once the deed is in your name, the deal with those KOWPIE people can easily be revoked." He sat back in his chair and crossed his legs, resting his pudgy hands on the arms.

"I can see the place needs work. I'd like to take care of some immediate needs, like the bathroom and some of the upstairs windows, maybe the roof, before I decide about selling."

"You're wasting your time and money if the purchaser has no need of the buildings."

Judy fought down a feeling of revulsion over the man's coldhearted statement. "There's something else that was brought to my attention. A business arrangement I'm not sure you were aware of."

Reynolds suddenly sat upright in his chair with renewed interest. "Oh?"

"Yes." Judy glanced down at the purse on her lap then back up. "Mr. Wingate and Aunt Louise had an agreement about the stock. He's bringing a paper to me later with the details."

Reynolds twisted in the chair, tapping a pencil against his chin. "Okay. You're right; that wasn't part of the report. I'll have to see that paperwork, if you don't mind. Let me reiterate that remodeling might be a waste of resources."

"Thank you. I appreciate your advice, but a girl's gotta have some comfort. I don't know how Aunt Louise could stand using that dinky little bathroom." Judy rose from the chair and reached to press his hand. "Thank you for your time. I'll just stop at the market while I'm in town. You have my cell number, right?"

Reynolds followed her to the door. "You can get around town all right? The market's up one block and over two. City Hall's on the right, and the library, such as it is, is out four blocks to the right and up one block, on West Street, across from the newspaper office—the *Robertsville Reporter*. Comes out twice a week. There you go."

Judy drove slowly to the little town market. She wheeled her wire grocery buggy around the market's tight, shallow aisles and nearly toppled a display of canned goods. Despite the lackluster atmosphere, Carl's Market felt homey. Neighbors who apparently frequented the place greeted each other warmly and shared bits of gossip. Heavenly odors wafted from the bakery section. Mounds of bananas filled a tub in the middle of produce. Judy rounded a corner where she came cart-to-cart with Ardyth Belters.

"Why, hello, Ardyth." Judy stared at the dizzying pattern of daisies adorning the black and yellow plaid check of the woman's jacket.

Ardyth nodded at Judy's cart. "So, you outlasted the casserole crowd?"

Judy smiled in appreciation of the joke. "Almost."

"Have you heard from the coroner yet?"

"No. I've been keeping in touch with the sheriff's department, too. They've been very kind. I wanted you to know that I'll be going back to Lewiston on Saturday. . .just for the day to pack some of my things. Maybe Bryan could feed Carranza and pick up the mail for me."

"I'll make a note of that, dear. We'll set up a tea date when you get back." Ardyth waved and took her basket of produce toward the front of the store.

After Judy finished her shopping and drove up to the house, the peace and quiet of a summer at the farm while she worked on her research brought on a sense of well-being. Just the scents and sounds of the farm and uninterrupted time would comfort her.

Judy stopped on the threshold of the back door of the farmhouse with her bag of groceries. A warm gust smelling of cut clover washed over her. If she sold, she wouldn't be able to visit anymore. This farm had been in the family well over a hundred years. She could hear the hum of the tractor from behind the barn, which meant Hart was nearby. *Now, why wouldn't I sell?*

Judy noticed the red light of the answering machine. Greves had returned Bryce's original call, eager to make an appointment to assess her remodeling job. Curious about Clyde Greves since she'd read the newspaper clipping, she placed her own call before hauling in the groceries from her trunk. Roxanne Greves patched

Judy through to her husband's phone at his current job site.

"Miss Winters?"

"Yes." Judy awkwardly cradled the unfamiliar width and length of the old-fashioned receiver.

"Ma'am, Bryce Edwards thought you could be using my services. Tell the truth, I been itchin' to get at that place out there for years. Such good, natural woodwork. Shame to see so much paint covering the character. Hmm, anyway. I've had a cancellation, I'm sure you've heard, and I'd be pleased to make your acquaintance."

Tickled at his turn of phrase, she thought she'd better get used to being "ma'am'd."

"I'm delighted to hear that, Mr. Greves. Whenever you could come and look over the place, I'll be here."

"Oh, I'm just Clyde, ma'am."

Clyde declared his intent to come out right away since he was only another coat of varnish from finishing his current job. He'd be packing up for the afternoon while the current application dried.

Clyde's Repairs graced each side of the faded tomato soup–colored van Judy met in the driveway. The man bounded from his van, pointed-toed, spit-shined, black leather cowboy boots first. Judy expected a ten-gallon hat to follow, but it was just Clyde's hair, a halo of a faded brown scrub brush and a matching rumpled mustache. Clyde's thick wire-rimmed glasses were nearly opaque, but he seemed to not miss a thing. From a distance, she couldn't tell that he rose no higher than her own five-feet-five inches and was startled when they shook hands, nose to nose.

"Howdy-do, Miss Judy," Clyde said, giving her hand a vigorous shake. "We are all so saddened by Louise's passing."

"Um, th–thank you." A mental image of Clyde holding a cowboy hat across his chest in an expression of sorrow flashed in front of her. Judy swallowed and pressed her lips firmly together. "Where would you like to start?"

"Why don't you tell me what you have in mind, and then I'll inspect ev'rthing."

Judy led the way into the kitchen. Clyde turned his head to get a full picture of the place while she sat him down, poured out the indispensable coffee, and told him what she wanted.

"I know you aren't a plumber," Judy said, winding down her plans.

"Nope, but my nephew is." Clyde twitched his mustache. "He's been put on notice. I do recall that little bit of a broom closet for a bathroom Harold and Una had." He nodded down the hall. "Thataway, if I'm not mistaken. Yep, that'll have to be taken care of. We can give her a look-see, and determine where you might expand."

Clyde gazed up at the nine-and-a-half-foot ceilings. "House like this was made for nat'ral air conditioning," he commented. "High ceilings, vents down low." He pointed out the overhang of an unused stairway to the basement and a little nook that might have been a solarium back in the day. "You can break through, here." He squinted. "And here."

"I agree—that would work out just fine to bump out the bathroom so a body can turn around in it," Judy said, delighted with his concept. "I don't use that space under the stairs. I wondered about the order of doors and transom windows throughout the place. I'm beginning to realize how clever the builders were."

Clyde sucked his teeth and continued on. "And the high, open staircase made for warm air to rise, you know."

Judy nearly bumped into him when he stopped abruptly at the bottom of the steps in the main hall to see if she paid attention. Satisfied, he continued outside to the front porch.

"Yep, replace the railing, obviously, some o' the floor here and where the eaves got plugged, and let the water down here."

Judy kept up with him but remained silent during the rest of his inspection.

"No termites, anyway. That's a blessing. I can get the ball movin', say, by Friday afternoon. I can bring supplies in. Give you a chance to check into obtaining the proper permits. I s'pose somebody told you about the inspections—well and septic. Prob'ly have to have the septic pumped. . ." He shook his head, as if the bearer of no good news. "Say, I also gotta warn you, it'll be powerful dusty. I vacuum, but you'll want to keep up, too."

"I intend to do my share of work," Judy said. "Whatever I can to help."

Clyde slapped his thigh and ambled to the van. "Well, I like that!"

So what if Clyde had convictions about saving

trees in his younger years? Showed he cared. Judy hadn't detected a whit of disingenuousness in his attitude and was delighted to engage his services upon recommendations from his former customers and his quotes.

———

Judy's trip to Lewiston coincided perfectly with Clyde's plan to break through the bathroom wall.

In one of those middle-of-the-night brainstorms, she decided she wanted to do everything she could to tackle the mystery of Louise's death. Packing up and returning to Lewiston and cashing in on the family farm without another thought just didn't feel right. Louise's murderer had not stolen anything that Judy could pinpoint. That left a motive that appeared to be based on the acquisition of the farmland. Or possibly a horde of gold.

Suspects? How could she even begin to accuse people she didn't know? Truth be told, the people who had the most to gain so far were the Reynoldses and Bryce Edwards. Bryce had been out of town at the time of Louise's death—or so he said. Judy could hardly bear the thought of the kindly man doing anything so heinous. Of course, he could have had an accomplice, one who had access to the farm. Mr. Wingate fit that picture. Judy sighed. She had better pay attention to the cattle deal he said he'd made with Louise. She needed to study KOWPIE. Hobart? Judy's intuition said no. A measly forty acres, or a sixteenth of a section, didn't have heinous attractions about it out here where farms constituting at least a half section of township were the norm. Unless that forty hid something special.

On the morning she went to Lewiston, she set a goal for her summer on the farm. By the middle of August, if she could determine whether Louise died because of some accident or of natural causes, well, there was nothing further to be gained by keeping the farm. She would be able to sell and move back to her life in Lewiston. If, however, she had the slightest doubt that Louise died of natural causes, she vowed to do all she could to figure out who and why and stay on the farm in order to keep the family heritage intact.

She would start with the one man who believed her aunt's death was unnatural: Chief Barry Hutchinson. Judy made a quick phone call to the station to set up an appointment with the chief early next week when she returned from Lewiston. In the meantime, he said he'd gather what information he could on the group known as KOWPIE. If the developer, Country Estates LLC, was legitimate, she shouldn't have trouble pulling any public records about them. Hobart could wait. The treasure and getting Bryce to talk might take some finesse.

To Judy, all the gold in the world wasn't worth the cost of her aunt's life, accident or not.

5

At times Judy's mind raced faster than the car did during the two-hour drive along the lovely Wisconsin River to Lewiston.

She unlocked the door to her apartment and waved her hand to dispel the stale air. She set her bag on the blue armchair in the living room and glanced around. Where was that homey feel? Judy turned a slow circle, staring at the apartment as though she were a stranger. This place didn't feel like home right now; it was odd how the farmhouse did. How could a house she had merely visited as a child feel more like home than the apartment she'd lived in for the past two years?

She methodically took care of mail and messages then decided to cancel the newspaper and forward her mail. "What else?" Judy said as she gathered clothes and other personal items. "Plants, laptop. . ." she murmured as she gathered files she didn't want to leave behind. How do you pack for a two-month murder investigation?

Help me sort out my grief and anger, Lord, Judy prayed, before steeling herself for the visit to Graham. What could she accomplish by getting him to admit he'd come to visit Louise without telling her? What could he have possibly wanted from her aunt that he had to hide it from her?

Graham's condo was a ten-minute drive away through town. He waited for her outside the front entrance. "Judy! Did you miss me? Come on, I've got some cheese and crackers. I have to leave in about an hour, you know."

Judy followed him inside. Graham decorated his apartment with souvenirs from his travels to the southwest and Mexico, the Caribbean, and other South American adventures. She set her purse down and accepted a tall glass of iced tea.

"Come, sit," he invited. "You look serious."

She decided to jump right in. "Someone in Robertsville thought he saw you there. Before the funeral. I wasn't with you."

Graham took a long drink. He reached forward to the coffee table and carefully built a tower of summer sausage and cheese on a cracker. He took a bite before meeting her gaze. "He? A man told you this?"

Graham used that hesitation trick in an attempt to hide his physical reaction to her accusation. Turning her question into one of his own put her on the defensive.

"It doesn't matter who saw you, Graham. Only that someone did."

"You're obviously concerned."

"Don't try that psychobabble on me. You're not denying it?"

"I went to Robertsville."

"Why?" Judy's breaths came faster. "And why not tell me?"

"I had some business there. Then, when you and I started going out and I knew your aunt wasn't all that crazy about me, I just wanted. . ." Graham tossed the cracker on the table. "Judy, I just wanted her to get to know me a little better. Show her I could be. . .good enough. You know. . .for you."

Judy examined every little pulse, every tiny twitch, the fluctuations of his hazel irises, and told herself he meant it. Ashamed, she cleared her throat. "Graham." She reached for his hand. "You should have said something."

Graham heaved himself to his feet and went to the open patio door. She got up and followed, watching her reflection approach his larger one. Her head reached just past his shoulder. Strands of her hair ruffled in the breeze.

"You don't trust me." Graham's voice was flat. Emotionless. "Just tell me, what makes me such a—a. . . villain in your eyes? In Louise's eyes? Huh?" He turned and took her shoulders. "I'll do anything, Judy. Just tell me, what can I do to make you trust me? I'm the one who knows what's best for you."

"What are you talking about? What do you mean, 'what's best for me'?"

His gaze pinned her. "Don't you believe that I want what's best for you? For us?"

Judy took a step back. "Graham, why did Louise ask you to leave? I want an answer."

Graham released his tight hold on her. "I asked her about her plans for the farmland. I thought that maybe it would make a nice place for us, after. . .you know. . ."

"After what?"

The phone rang, and Graham's mouth made a grim line. He began to herd her toward the front door. "After we're married, of course."

"What? We hardly—"

"I'm sorry your aunt's gone and sorry we can't talk more now." He opened the door. "You know, I just remembered that I have to be to work a little early today. We're doing some inventory. I'll call—"

"Married? Graham, I'm not prepared to discuss anything like that yet. In fact, I'm going back to the farm today. I'm having some remodeling done."

"What for? We don't need that old house. The land is what's. . ." The phone started up again. "Listen, I'll call you later, babe."

Judy barely had the foresight to grab her purse from the table near the door. And with that, she found herself staring at the closed door, the click of the lock echoing down the hallway.

Judy raced the sunset back to the farm, arriving just as the red ball sunk behind the hills of western Wisconsin. A solitary dinner and a movie was all she needed to help her relax.

She awoke the next morning in the television room tucked into the snuggly afghan, cell phone clutched in hand. No messages blinked for attention. Glad? Or Sad? Graham had spouted the word *marriage* and then dismissed her. Maybe she'd imagined the whole conversation. Once she might have considered Graham Montgomery potentially marriageable, but his actions yesterday unnerved her. His poutiness and lack of support for her desire to settle her aunt's estate cast a poor light on his character. But she couldn't just write off Graham, either. The stress of the funeral and trying to untangle Aunt Louise's will might be clouding her judgment. She'd let Graham make the next move.

Judy stretched. It was long past making ten o'clock worship. Ah, well, next week. Being able to plan for church and the future pleased her.

There were plenty of things to occupy her time today, including claiming a bedroom. Clyde had set up a screened-off portable toilet in a corner behind the porch. Small favors.

After a light lunch, which she carried out and ate on the swept front porch, Judy tackled the monumental task of cleaning ancient layers of grease and flyspecks off the kitchen ceiling. She intended to repaint after Clyde was done. Mixed-in remodeling dust with the flyspecks would only make her task harder later on. Judy dragged a ten-foot aluminum ladder from the garage. She struggled with the awkward length, hauling the thing through the mudroom and then into the kitchen.

Because of the strange angle between the solarium part of the room, which was divided by a rounded arch and the cupboards, she faced a dilemma. She decided to lean the folded-up ladder against the corner cabinet. Bracing the end with a chair or heavy box might add stability but would get in the way of her climbing down. She rested the top against the buttress of the wall divider, testing the position a few times with a cautious jiggle. Satisfied the ladder would stay in place, Judy grabbed a bucket of soapy water and climbed up, humming to herself. Heights she could deal with; falling was another story. She whooped when she found she could reach into the corner.

"This room really is a shiny white. Maybe I won't have to repaint the whole thing," Judy muttered, assessing her handiwork out loud.

"What was that?" Hart's voice came through the screen door. "Hello!" he called and opened the door.

Judy twisted around at the top of ladder, hanging precariously for an instant before she lost her balance. The bucket went first.

"Hey! Look out!" she managed to call out, before she began her unplanned descent in what felt like slow motion. She had time to notice the most peculiar expression, mixed surprise and rue, on Hart's face as he dodged the falling bucket and kept his footing while dirty water and the washrag splashed up against his jeans. He had one hand on the ladder and managed to thrust his back under her just as she came hurtling down on top of him. The ladder slid slowly until it came to rest against the table.

"Thank you," Judy said in a small voice, draped over the prone figure of her neighbor, whose face pressed into the filthy puddle on the floor.

"You're welcome." He didn't move except to test his voice. "Are you hurt?"

Judy realized that she had not moved either and, embarrassed, rolled away and sat up. She raised her eyes toward the clean spot she'd scrubbed, noting how far she fell. "Well, thanks to you, I'm not hurt, but you probably are. Don't. . ."

Hart untangled himself from her legs and twisted himself out of the puddle. He wiped at his face as he sat up. He stretched his shoulders and shook his head then cautiously got to his feet, a hand to his gut. He took in a shallow breath and winced. "I'll live." He gave the ladder his attention then glanced back at her. "Just what were you doing up there, with the ladder not set properly?"

His eyes are brown. He's not wearing those stupid sunglasses, so I can tell. She stood, twisting her mouth. "I'm so sorry. I was just cleaning the ceiling, getting ready to repaint—"

"You?"

"I can paint!" Judy's fists came to rest on her hips as she glared at him.

Hart swiveled his head around the kitchen and then to her. "I'm picturing a can of paint, splattered all over the floor and the cabinets, and you lying here on the floor."

"Thank you for your concern."

Hart took in another shallow breath and paled. He reached a hand down to dust off his jeans but quickly straightened again and clutched his midriff.

Judy started forward, but he indicated the manila folder he'd tossed on the kitchen table. "There. That's the agreement between Louise and me. We never had the contract notarized or anything like that, but we both signed on the purchase of the original twelve head, although she used her own money. I agreed to see to the care and breeding, and the offspring would be mine."

Judy hadn't taken her eyes off him, concerned about his stillness. She carried on her inspection, ignoring his statement for the time being. He was pleasant to look at, nice cheekbones, although one bore a red mark, and smooth-shaven square jaw. Judy glanced away when she noticed a little scrap of paper or leaf or something stuck, drying, to the side of his chin.

"I'll, ah, talk to Mr. Reynolds about this, and the county agricultural agent, but I believe you. I don't have any reason not to." Judy began to move the chair closest to her in toward the table. Without looking at him, she stuck out her hand in his direction. "Thank you for dropping by and for rescuing me. I'm glad you weren't hurt. I will do all that I can to honor your agreement."

Hart gave her hand one firm squeeze and dropped it. They moved together slowly to the back door. He grimaced. "You're welcome. We'll be in touch."

"You're sure you're all right? Maybe we should—"

"No. I'm okay."

"Well, good-bye, then," Judy said to his back, as he let the screen door close.

After her supper, she realized her neck muscles felt stiff. She didn't hurt enough to make a visit to a doctor, but she wondered how Hart felt. She'd hit him pretty hard when she fell. *He walked out of here just fine,* Judy reminded herself. Still, she considered calling him. Her own telephone rang first, with an invitation from Bryce to Bible study at church.

"I noticed you weren't with us to worship today," Bryce said. "Ardyth mentioned you were thinking of going to Lewiston, so I wasn't worried. I realize now that I should have been, though, with you all alone out there."

"How thoughtful of you. I appreciate the invitation. Clyde Greves will be here during the day, though."

"I'm glad he was able to start right in. So, would you like to attend? We meet on Wednesday evenings. I'll take you out for a snack afterward, introduce you to some of the fine dining establishments we have to offer."

"Of course I'd love to join you. Six o'clock, then?"

"Perfect," Bryce said.

"And thank you for offering to pick me up."

Judy hung up, wondering if she could find a polite way to ask Bryce about his supposed lost Alaskan treasure.

Judy yanked open the closet door of her bedroom. Still in the throes of cleaning, she stamped her foot when she heard a little scrabbling noise from behind the wall of her bed. Mice.

"Carranza!" Where was that animal now that she wanted him? Judy leaned out of the doorway, scanning both directions of the spacious upstairs hall. During a prosperous era of farming and settling, the Jamisons had built a large home in hopes of filling it with offspring. Unfortunately, the family never raised to adulthood more than two or three children in one era; more often one child was sole heir in the next generation. No wonder heritage had been so important to Louise.

Six square bedrooms with the luxury of built-in closets flowed off a large central hall, complete with a wide stairway and landing on either end. Judy chose a room near the steps to the kitchen, contemplated the decadence of building a full bathroom upstairs at some point, and called the cat again.

"Carranza! Mice!" This time she heard padding along the hall as the mouser answered her summons. He cocked his head in the direction of the open door and leaped inside. A hiss and a squeak later, Carranza regally presented Judy with her boon.

Carranza set the thing at her feet and waited.

"Um, thank you." Judy tried to use the same wheedling voice Ardyth had. "You can take it away now."

Carranza strutted off minus his catch.

Certain the beastly cat only pretended not to understand and obey her order, Judy got out the broom and dustpan and shoveled the mouse's body out the window.

"I'm living on a farm," Judy said as she climbed into bed. Better to dwell on the harmless creatures than on being alone at night. At least the excitement of the day had kept her from reflecting on the visit to Chief Hutchinson on the morrow.

Promptly at seven thirty the next morning, Judy opened the door for Clyde and his assistant, a silent giant of a young man introduced as Chet.

By ten fifty, Judy drove off, glad to get away from the sound of home improvement. She drove into Robertsville, where she'd arranged to have coffee with the chief at Colette's Counter, the local sandwich shop in the two-block segment that served as Robertsville's downtown.

Dressed in a brown-and-tan uniform with a sparkling badge, Barry Hutchinson exuded comfort and authority. "Miss Winters. . .Judy. Thank you for coming." His warm handshake and the fatherly twinkle in his eyes put her at ease.

After they settled into a booth and placed their orders, Chief Hutchinson said, "I have all the information I could dredge up on KOWPIE. We in law enforcement have a tag on that group."

Judy tilted her head. "Tag?"

"Just our term for spotting potential troublemakers. Up in the deep woods there are a lot of places to stay out of sight."

"Aunt Louise raised me on stories of Al Capone and his gang hiding out during prohibition." Judy watched him steadfastly, intent on decoding his facial expressions.

Hutchinson chuckled. "That's right. I don't know how different some of these groups are, but—"

"Here we go." Colette brought them mugs of coffee and a couple of her cinnamon rolls, along with an order to call her if they needed anything else.

"As I was saying. . ." Hutchinson took a swallow of black coffee. "Seems there's always someone bent on trouble. Don't want to pay their fair share of taxes but expect the same rights as those who do. They think they can do whatever they please with a gun and not worry about the consequences. Folks like that don't seem to care that they pose a threat to innocent people." He shook his head. "Anyway, I can tell you some of the things we know about this particular group. Some of the information is classified, of course." Hutchinson peered at her with a lack of pretension she found touching.

"Of course." Judy pulled off a piece of warm cinnamon bun. "Thank you. Do you have any names?"

The chief took a huge bite of the bun and then another gulp of coffee. "Some. I can't quite pin down why, but I have the feeling that there's another person who's calling the shots, who doesn't live on the compound they have up near Rice Lake."

"Why's that?"

"We can account for pretty near a dozen men and women, about your age, no kids, coming and going. Seems like each has a particular job—like taking care of food, yard work, and the like. They run a mechanical repair business to raise cash. Go to protests, even organize some, I guess, like banning pesticides or the chemicals used in lakes to keep the weeds down. There's no telephone service that we can determine, so they must use some sort of wireless service. And that leads me to why I think there's at least one person on the outside."

"Rice Lake's sort of far from here."

Hutchinson drank from the chunky ceramic mug, grimaced, and added sugar. Judy waited in silence, noting the interplay of emotions working across the chief's face. He needed to decide what and how much to tell her. She respected the difficulty of his position.

"Pelican Creek has a similar group, and so does Big Bear Lodge." Hutchinson named two communities, mostly seasonal tourist haunts, between Robertsville and Rice Lake. He met Judy's look openly. "Frankly, we think they want to spread out. When Ardyth Belters came to me after Louise's death and told me that she thought Louise was afraid of somebody, I personally contacted the county sheriff, Danner, and relayed the info." The man's dismay oozed from every pore. "I don't usually feel as helpless as I did looking down at that poor woman's body. I'm just as puzzled as anyone to why she died. She was my age, too—fifty-four. Nerve-racking."

"Do you think that once we know the type of poison, we'll nab whoever did it?"

"Hard to say. I hope so, I certainly do, but Danner hasn't ruled out accident. . .yet."

"You don't think Hart Wingate had anything to do with Louise's death?" The heat of a blush burned her face. What if the chief was reading *her* signals? Judy cleared her throat. "I mean, Hart seemed to be genuinely sorry about her."

Hutchinson nodded. "He's been cooperative, from what I understand. He has a solid alibi and nothing to gain, either, am I right? Louise's will didn't mention him in any way?"

"No, nothing at all in her will." Judy felt hopeful. The last person she wanted to suspect was Hart. "Well, except for a weird little business deal with cows on the side. But, honestly, he had a good deal even before my aunt's death."

A deep line formed between the chief's brows. "Cows?"

"Yeah. Aunt Louise bought some cattle, and they agreed that he would take care of them, buy feed and that, and then he'd keep the calves in exchange."

"Hmm. Okay." Hutchinson tapped the table with his spoon. "You feel comfortable with that?"

"Sure do," she spoke a tad too quickly. "Seems up and up. He helped Aunt Louise a lot. As far as information about Country Properties, the company is owned by Gene and Laura Reynolds. They developed the Sunny Heights subdivision. I couldn't pull up any complaints or Better Business Bureau issues. In my opinion, Gene Reynolds just wants to make money and Louise's farm is on his list of acquisitions. According to him, the property is worth quite a bit of money. He said it's enough to make me independent, so my aunt's land must mean a lot more to him."

Hutchinson's cheeks pooched inward. *All the classic signs of determination. But toward what end?*

"I'll make sure there's a regular patrol by your place at night, Judy, even if I have to drive past on my breaks."

A sinking feeling hit the pit of her stomach. "You think I should be worried?" Judy's appetite vanished, and she abandoned the remainder of the cinnamon roll.

"In a small community like this, everyone knows you're alone out there. Wouldn't hurt."

"If anything happens to me—"

"We'll make sure nothing does, ma'am."

Judy winced. "Thanks. The property seems to be the issue here. I suppose I wouldn't do wrong by having a will of my own drawn up. Oh, and Ardyth Belters told me she thought Aunt Louise was going to change her mind about her will."

Despair. Judy couldn't be mistaken at the chief's display of emotion. Lines appeared between his eyebrows.

"She did?"

She had the feeling that wasn't news to him. "If the person who stands the most to gain from getting the land knows that I made specific arrangements, I should be safe, right?"

Curiosity. One of Chief's eyebrows subtly lifted, and the tiny right tilt of his chin was the classic sign. "Could be." He shifted his legs to reach his wallet. Judy watched him draw out a business card, which he offered to her. "Can I make a suggestion?" He didn't wait for a response. "Here's the name of my lawyer. She's good. Would you consider using her services if you do have a will made? And I'll just have a quiet word with the Reynoldses. Both of them."

She wasn't about to commit yet, so she settled on a new topic. "So now we wait for the toxicology report?"

"We wait," Hutchinson confirmed.

⚊

Bryce came to collect Judy for Wednesday evening Bible study, as he promised. She and Bryce prayed together for God to anoint the group before driving into town.

As soon as they entered the conference room in the church, Bryce went to say hello to other acquaintances. Judy discovered that her neighbor, Hart, also attended the study. Perhaps in the future they could come together. Or, maybe not, judging by the way he sat ram-rod straight, pale-faced, and quiet in his chair at the long table with the other dozen or so members of the Bible study group. Pastor Tyson was teaching a series of lessons that would take them through the book of Hebrews.

Pastor spoke on making worship a part of daily life. "Based on Jesus' teaching in Luke 6:9, I ask you, which is lawful on the Sabbath: to do good or to do evil, to save life or to destroy it? Jesus didn't limit his ministry to the Sabbath, so we shouldn't, either."

The session concluded, and Judy was determined to catch up with Hart before he left. Bryce followed in her wake. Judy reached out her hand to Hart and touched his shoulder. "Listen, I'm so sorry. I must have really hurt you," she said.

Bryce cocked his head, and Judy hastened to explain. "Hart literally caught me when I fell from the ladder in the kitchen on Sunday afternoon."

Bryce coughed and began to move away. "I'll meet you in the hall for that tour later."

Hart turned his head and whispered out of the corner of his mouth, "Just a couple of cracked ribs. They're taped and will heal up fast. Don't worry."

Judy gasped. "Cracked ribs?"

"Do *not* make a production out of this," Hart mumbled, as he led the way to the hall.

Bryce stood out there and began to hum as he examined a magazine in a wall rack.

"There you are!" A feminine voice called out.

Judy turned and tried to smile.

"I saw you the other day in Carl's. Are you planning to stay around, then? Remember me, Mary Tennison? And this is my husband, Ralph."

Judy recognized several faces, if not names, from her past visits to church and the funeral. "Hello, Mrs. Tennison. It's nice to meet you again."

Bryce grinned from dimple to dimple when he joined the group, covering Hart's escape. He winked at Judy.

Mary seemed to be the chief spokesperson. "Call me Mary," she invited. "Why, your uncle Harold was a fine man. Una, too, of course. She's been gone quite awhile, now, though. Harold was a trustee here at church, you know. My Ralph took his place when he passed. Not that anyone could really take his place. And Louise. Poor Louise. What a shame." Mary introduced the others.

"Who'll nag us to pick up aluminum cans now?" Ralph Tennison moaned, obviously mocking by the gleam in his eye.

Mary elbowed her husband. "Hush. Don't speak ill of the dead."

"Harold and Una were part of our group," Ruth Harris said, ignoring the theatrics of the Tennisons. "We used to get together and play cards every other week. We had such a good time. A regular tradition."

"We'd have holiday gatherings, too. Potlucks and parties," petite Betty St. George added. Her tall, bushy-haired husband, Tom, talked about jerry-rigging equipment on the farm. "We got so caught up in fixing things that we had a competition to see who could figure out how to keep Harold's old hay baler running the longest with the least amount of parts." The men chortled.

"Art, here, though, takes the prize for originality," Tom said when the geniality died down.

"Oh?" Art Harris asked, a perpetually startled expression on his weather-lined face.

Tom laughed. "The amazing bomb shelter you built, of course!"

Judy watched Bryce's eyes go wide with recognition.

"Yeah, say," Art said, "isn't that where little Louise hid your gold nuggets, Edwards?"

"Ahem." Bryce cleared his throat, giving the men a waggly eyebrow warning.

"Judy will have a chance to look for them, then, won't she?" Betty said.

"So, are you staying on, dear?" Mary asked again.

"Just for the summer," Judy said, backing up a bit. The barrage of questions made her uncomfortable. "You know I'm a teacher."

Ruth crossed her arms. "That's right. Louise spoke of you often. Maybe they could find you a job right here. Then you wouldn't ever have to leave."

"That Ardyth!" Mary apparently just noticed that Ardyth had scurried from the room as soon as Pastor Tyson said "Amen." "She's done her disappearing act again. Whatever is the matter with that girl?"

Judy heard Bryce's intake of breath. "If you folks don't mind, I promised I'd show Judy around." He took Judy's elbow, and they made a hurried circuit around the upper level of the square limestone building. "Sanctuary. You've seen that, of course. Library, kitchenette, offices. Back door. Let's go to the diner for some dessert."

Bryce led her outside and settled her into the passenger side of his car. He got in and closed his door. As Judy turned to buckle her seat belt, she caught sight of Ardyth walking at a determined pace toward the back parking lot, head thrust forward. Judy checked Bryce's tight-mouthed profile. Curious.

At the pleasant family restaurant just outside of town near the freeway, Judy leaned back in her chair, cradling a cup of coffee in both hands.

"I wondered what happened to make Hart walk so tenderly," Bryce commented, after pouring himself a warm-up out of the carafe.

"I'm just mortified," Judy confessed. "I leaned the ladder on purpose so I could reach the corner. I was nearly done when Hart came in. He startled me, and I lost my balance. He broke my fall. I guess that wasn't all he broke. He said he has some cracked ribs. How can I make it up to him?"

"He's an independent type, in case you haven't noticed. But just the same, you and I can help with chores for a week, can't we?"

"Of course," Judy said. "That's the least I can do. So, did I hear right? Art built a bomb shelter on the farm? Where is it?"

Bryce picked up his fork and examined it. "Well, that's a good tale," he said. "You may not be aware of how scared some people were during the Cold War."

Judy nodded. "I teach about it in Social Studies."

"Ancient history. I suppose you do. All that happened before you were born, of course. But there were a lot of nervous people at the time." He shook his head. "Your aunt Una, whose family lived through World War II in Sweden, became so fearful. She convinced your uncle that they needed a bomb shelter. Harold ordered a kit, and Art there improved the plans. I know the bunch of 'em joked about making the thing big enough for a good dozen people, but they meant no harm. Built it right in the backyard. Some folks thought Harold foolish, but he made Una happy."

"Nothing I can see in the backyard looks like a bomb shelter."

"I suppose after the threat was over, they didn't think much about the shelter anymore. Until little Louise came along and found the opening. Wanted to play. Of course, her mother was horrified and determined to have the thing backfilled."

"So did they?" She restrained herself from asking about the possibility of hidden treasure.

"Not entirely. That was the year Una found out she was sick. You want to know about the rumors, don't you? There's lost treasure? I suppose Louise told you."

"Ardyth Belters told me."

Bryce's eyebrows shot up. "Oh. That explains why you'd be reluctant to talk to me."

"I've noticed that Ardyth doesn't act as though she feels comfortable around you."

Their server set slices of pecan pie in front of them. Judy licked her lips.

Bryce sampled his then turned his coffee cup in his calloused hands. "When I was a foolish young man, I had dreams that were too big for me." He sighed. "Harold and I wanted an adventure. A treasure hunt. We also thought we each would settle down, eventually. Of course, we'd both marry and raise a family as long as we found a wife just like Ardyth—the sweetest, most fun girl we knew. But the three of us were friends first and foremost, and we didn't want to spoil that relationship. We made a pact, perhaps foolishly, but nevertheless an agreement of sorts, that whichever of us panned the most would get the first chance to court Ardyth."

He snorted then took another bite and chewed. "Well, Harold found his treasure, only it wasn't gold; it was Una. I came back from Alaska bearing gifts for my true love only to discover that she wasn't my true love after all. I don't know if she ever had been. She never answered my letters or talked to me, and she eventually moved away."

He drained his coffee cup. "Well, anyway, nothing meant much to me anymore, and I put my dreams away. I enjoyed the company of my best friend's family. One day my boss asked me to put on a machine training seminar down in San Antonio for seven months. Little Louise and I were good pals by then. I let her take my treasure chest, for a pledge, you know, that I would come back and reclaim it." Bryce smiled. "So she wouldn't feel bad about me leaving. The thing wasn't that big and was locked tight."

"And Louise lost your box."

"That's right. She told me she'd been afraid when her parents talked about the gypsies coming. She put my box in the bomb shelter for safekeeping. When I returned, we went to look." He shook his head. "No sign. Louise cried for days. I just assumed someone else found my gold."

Judy felt a chill run down her spine. "So you really had gold?"

Bryce nodded. "I never told Louise or Harold or Una how much gold. I didn't want them to feel bad for losing the box. I made the choice to entrust a little girl and lost my treasure. More to the point, the gold didn't mean anything to me anymore, not without the woman I loved to share it with me." He waved his hand. "Oh, and I don't blame Louise, either. I doubt we'll ever find out what happened. But, as a lark, before you sell the place, I'd sure like you and Hart to keep an eye out."

"Hart knows?"

"Well, yes. Since he's on my place just next door, I told him to poke around. You never know what clues you'll come across."

Judy scooted to the very end of her seat. "You said the gold didn't mean anything to you anymore. Just how valuable was your treasure?" A new boldness, born of her love for her aunt and a need to find the culprit, pushed her to speak her mind with confidence. "Valuable enough to kill Louise? Come on, Bryce. Why would anyone want to hurt her?"

A shadow crossed the table. "Evening folks," Red Hobart said. "Good pie, ain't it?"

"Hi, Red." Judy nodded a greeting. "How are you?"

"Fine. 'Cept I need to talk to you, Judy," Hobart replied. "When can I take possession of that there forty promised to my family?"

"I'm surprised at you, Hobart," Bryce said, "coming over like this to talk nonsense."

"As good a time as any, Edwards." Hobart returned his beady eyes to her. "So, Judy, how much longer before you sell?"

Her fingernails bit into her palms. Judy drew a deep breath. She couldn't allow Hobart or anybody else to ruffle her feathers if she expected to get to the truth. "I haven't decided on anything yet, Red. Aunt Louise wrote in her will that she wanted to give the farm to that KOWPIE group, but I'm not sure in my heart of hearts that's truly what she wanted. I'm studying all my options."

"KOWPIE!" Red jammed his hands in his overall pockets and wagged his head. "What a bunch of nonsense. I'll tell you something—"

"No, you won't, Hobart." Bryce threw down his napkin and pushed his chair away from the table. "You've already cut a new fence line a dozen feet on Judy's side, and you're not getting any more. You can hardly take care of what you do have, and everyone knows Louise let you get away on a promise of rent for years."

"That gully doesn't do either of us any good. Louise said that I—"

"You took advantage of Louise! Harold told you before—"

"Please!" Judy got to her feet with an anxious look at the patrons who were openly staring. She pressed her trembling palms together.

Bryce rose, too, glowering. He signaled for the check.

Hobart crossed his arms and stared while Bryce counted out the money.

Judy tossed a bill on the table for a tip and met Hobart's fury. "We should talk, Red. I want to know where you were the morning Aunt Louise was found."

Hobart stuck his thumbs through the straps of his

bibs and rocked back on his boot heels. "I already told the sheriff. It ain't none of your business, but seeing as how we have an audience, I'll lay this to rest once and for all. I was right here. Everyone can tell ya. I took my eggs over easy and read the morning news. Same as every morning. And may I add, I don't like what you're implying."

"Thanks for letting me know. I apologize for any unseemly accusation, but as you say, now the matter is laid to rest."

Bryce muttered under his breath.

"What's that, Edwards?" Hobart leered toward him. "Got something on your mind?"

"I said, 'No wonder you can't get a crop in.'"

Judy put a hand on Bryce's arm.

"Fer your information, planter needs some welding done. If you can get Art Harris to bring my equipment back, I'd be grateful."

"Mr. Hobart." Judy summoned her most placating tone. "I'd still like to talk to you. . .about the farm. But I want to do it in Mr. Reynolds's office."

Red nodded, glaring bullets at Bryce the whole time. "That's a deal, ma'am."

The next day Judy decided to prepare a casserole for Hart. She could check up on him, say thank you, and tell him that she and Bryce would take care of the cows for the next week. Maybe even ask advice about the chickens. Clyde and his nephew, Chet, were outside whaling away at the framework of a new wall for the expanded bathroom. Clyde came and went, measuring and muttering. Every so often the saw would whine.

About eleven o'clock Judy stood near the garage, cleaning off the rake she'd used in the yard, and Clyde approached.

"Ma'am." Clyde turned a billed cap around and around in his dusty hands. Even his hair stood stiff with tension.

"What's the matter, Clyde?"

"I'm mighty sorry to be the bearer of bad tidings and all."

"Clyde, tell me." Judy stared at her contractor. What had happened to make him so upset? Surely cutting a board the wrong size or even finding termites wouldn't cause the man this much anxiety.

"Your new w.c., um, water closet, ma'am. Me and Chet went to pack it in, but it's been damaged."

Judy snorted in relief. "That's all? Well, surely that happens, right? Even the most careful of folks can have accidents."

Clyde continued a tortured circuit of the hat.

"Clyde, I'm getting a vibe that the w.c., er, toilet bowl, isn't the whole problem."

"Well, ma'am, Judy, uh, normally I'd say the w.c. was in a box so we'd just take it back for replacement at the suppliers, but me and Chet, we checked her over real good last night in preparation for the big event today, and ma'am, it were a thing of beauty. Not a scratch on her. Today, well, we took her out of the box real careful. The tank's cracked nearly in two. There's a chip out of the base, too, like where sumbuddy maybe took a hammer."

"So you think someone deliberately vandalized my toilet? Last night while—while. . ." Judy leaned on a tool bench in the garage, feeling as though a mighty hand had turned down the gravity button. "We should call the sheriff."

"Under normal circumstances, I would say we just had ourselves a little accident. But, ma'am, we started missing tools almost from the first. I didn't want to worry you, and we packed up our kit careful ev'ry night after my good hammer walked away. I found her again later so I didn't say nothing, thinking mayhap you'd just borrowed it."

Judy's fright forgotten, she began to heat with indignation. Clyde must have felt it, for he held his hands up defensively and blinked rapidly behind the spotted lenses.

"Now, ma'am, I don't hold no grudge with borrowing. Sometimes a person forgets to put a thing back or doesn't realize a hammer didn't come from his own tool belt, so I don't care. It came back. I know now you got plenty of your own." He indicated the Peg-Board backing the workbench. "I know you woulda asked permission, too, so now, when I see the w.c.'s been damaged and my air gun is missing, I feel I got to report to you."

"Air gun? You didn't tell me that before." Judy led the way inside the house. She picked up the phone and dialed the county authorities.

The sheriff promised to send an officer to take a report. While they waited, Clyde and Chet took their lunch outside near the faded van.

After the deputy had taken Chet's sparsely worded worry that he thought he left the air gun and compressor outside the back door, still plugged into an outlet, Clyde suspended work for the rest of the day.

"I'll be ordering the new unit right away," he assured. "We'll get you taken care of as soon as we can, Miss Judy."

Carranza stayed in the barn during the loudest part of construction. Judy spied him that morning when she went to do the chores. When she began to take note of the various-sized batches of cats, some friendly but most wary, she started to get a hint of the extent of his family tree. Perhaps a visit to a vet should go on her duty list.

Judy closed up her house and drove to Hart's. He answered her knock at the back door. He looked at the dish in her hands and then at her face.

"Hello," Judy said. "I–I'm sorry to bother you. I suppose I should have called first, but I guess I don't have your number."

Hart continued to stand at the door.

"Anyway, this is for you." Judy shifted feet, uncomfortable with not being able to read past the curiosity in his expression. She held the dish in his direction.

"Oh, well, thanks," Hart finally said. "I'm sorry to keep you standing out there. I was surprised, I guess." He stood back and held the door open. "Come in."

Judy entered the boxy kitchen and set the dish on the table. Everything sparkled. A few dishes dried in a rack. Except for the newspaper scattered over the kitchen table and a used coffee cup, the room could have just had professional maid service.

"Wow. You're clean," Judy said and then closed her eyes. Could she ever stop saying dumb things?

"Thanks. I suppose Clyde's making a lot of dust at your place." Hart leaned against the counter.

"Yes, he is, just like he promised. But I wanted to say how sorry I am about—about breaking your ribs. Are you in much pain?"

"No." He shrugged his broad shoulders. "And they're cracked. Barely." He lifted his arms shoulder high. "I can hardly tell. And the alternative would have been even more unpleasant. For both of us." His smile crinkled the corners of his eyes. "I would have been traumatized for life to see you break your neck right before my gaze."

"Gee, thanks." Judy laughed. "Well, anyway, I thought the least I could do was check up on you and bring you supper. Bryce and I plan to help with the cattle, until. . .well, you can. Get back to it, that is." Judy took a deep breath and rocked forward on her toes.

Hart leaned over the dish and inhaled. "Smells good, like something from home. Thank you." He refocused on her face. "Would you care to join me?"

She'd merely intended to drop the hot dish off and go home, but she found herself saying yes before she realized that she'd opened her mouth. Hart's response was to get out two plates, silverware, and cups, which he handed to her.

Judy stood at the table, laden plates in hand. "So, where do you usually sit?"

"In the living room."

"I know what you mean. I've taken over Aunt Louise's little television room off the kitchen." She pointed the forks at the table. "So, do you want me to set the table?"

"Sure, go ahead. I've got some salad here." He poked his head in the refrigerator. "And some leftover focaccia. How's that?"

"Sounds better than what I'd get at my house."

He offered a prayer of thanksgiving before she could pick up a fork. Pleased, Judy smiled at him before helping herself to the bread.

Hart moved deliberately, she noticed, bracing himself, rotating to face the object directly before picking up anything or setting it down. She distracted herself by yakking about the bread after they were seated at the table.

"This focaccia is delicious. I don't know many single men who'd think about buying this."

Hart had a fork nearly to his mouth. He paused, raising his eyebrows. Then he looked at the forkful of chicken and beans and put it in his mouth.

Judy waited while he chewed and swallowed, wondering if he thought she was impolite or nosy. She couldn't decipher his expression. Careful, maybe, contemplative. But what could be so strange about her comment? He sat back, wiped his mouth on his napkin, and picked up his glass of water. "My sister-in-law, Margie, is a good cook. She takes cooking classes all the time. She taught my mother and me how to make different kinds of bread. Gives you a good workout. Except that I won't be making any for a few days. My ribs are too tender yet."

"You made this?"

"Yeah. Hey, your casserole is great. Thanks for bringing it over. You didn't have to." He reached for the saltshaker and helped himself liberally. Graham had done the same when he came to eat with her. So she forgot some salt? Food was food.

"I wanted to do something to make amends," Judy said, finishing off her portion. "This is nice. Sitting here talking, I mean." She stopped in mid-dip of the bread into the seasoned olive oil Hart had set out.

She closed her eyes and grimaced. "That didn't come out quite right."

Hart paused. "We didn't exactly start out on the right foot. It's been a little rough for me these last couple of years. Just when I thought things were turning around, Harold plows his last row. And Louise. . .well, it just doesn't seem fair." Hart threw his crumpled napkin on the table. "She wasn't just a business partner but a friend, someone to talk to." He shoved his chair back and carefully got to his feet. "Would you like some coffee?"

Judy watched his back, aware that she'd been allowed a few feet into the life of this man. She wondered more about him, whether he'd ever been married or why he was here, farming alone.

"Yes, thank you." She stood and began to gather their plates.

"How do you like your coffee?"

"Black, thanks." Hart handed her a cup without comment and led the way into the sparsely furnished living room.

"Two more cows are ready to calve soon," Hart said. "I have a ways to go cleaning out the barn here and getting the stalls laid out how I want them."

Judy sat in his one slipcovered side chair while he carefully lowered himself to a cushion of a matching brown sofa. A couple of crates serving as a coffee tables completed the furnishings. "You won't be able to do any heavy work for a few weeks, I know, and I'm sorry. But Bryce will help, or maybe Bryan, Ardyth's grandson, can come."

"It won't be that long. Just a few days and I'll be good as new. Yeah, Bryan could use up some of that energy. Good idea. I'll call him. Bryce was here yesterday, too, looking over plans for the barn."

Judy felt the warmth of Hart's brown eyes and risked a change of subject. "I'd like to know your honest opinion about my aunt's death. No one wants to believe that Aunt Louise was killed deliberately. Who would do such a thing, anyway?"

"I don't know."

"But you must have an opinion. What did the police talk to you about?"

Hart got to his feet again with only a thinning of lips to indicate his painful ribs. He went to stand at the large window overlooking the main road. "They asked me about visitors, if I noticed anything unusual, that sort of thing. Who was mad at Louise now, if anybody. You know, she did kind of upset people whenever she saw anybody throwing cans away. And she went to every town board meeting to nag about recycling." He heaved a sigh. "Also about whether or not we'd set out any rat poison. What kind of feed and vitamins we give the cattle. If we used hormones." He turned to face her across the room. "I told them about your boyfriend's visit."

Judy stared at the cover of *Farmer's Co-op* magazine on the coffee table for all the diversion was worth. Conflicting feelings assailed her. She dated Graham. He was far from the ideal boyfriend. . .but murder her aunt? She shook her head.

"Judy? I'm sorry."

Judy met his dark eyes. "It's all right. You had to be honest with the police. I talked to Graham about it, too. He said he came to talk to Aunt Louise about. . .us. He said he hoped to convince my aunt to like him."

"You believe him?"

"I don't have any reason not to."

"Why didn't Louise like Graham?" Hart shook his head. "Sorry, that's none of my business."

"No, that's all right. I didn't think Louise disliked

him, really. It was more about Graham's perception of most people." Judy shrugged. "Graham said something about having business in Robertsville. But that reminds me—he never told me what his business in Robertsville was about." She scrambled to her feet. "Hart, do you know anything about Red building a fence on my side of the gully?"

"Louise knew what he did, Judy. It was on the quarter section that was supposed to go to the Hobarts when the Jamisons sold out, so Louise didn't care that much."

"I only heard about this promise since reading the will."

"Bryce was the one who first let me know when I told him about Red's fencing on your land. The deal has to do with something in the past, when the first Jamisons and Hobarts settled in the area. Something about how the Hobarts did a favor for the Jamisons. You'd have to ask Bryce."

"Red and I have an appointment to talk in a couple of days. You don't think he tried to collect early, do you?"

"By killing Louise? Red's not that kind of guy."

"Why would Red want that land? He hasn't paid the rent he owes and hasn't even planted yet."

Hart shrugged. "Red thought hi-tech would cover for his. . .lack of ability, I guess. He put up some outrageous new waste system and a huge down payment on that fancy tractor. Not a genius, that one. Can't harvest anything if you don't buy seed and actually plant it. He had to sell off most of his herd last fall."

"But I saw cattle in his pasture by the drive."

"Neighbor's."

"If he's so cash-poor, maybe he's taking stock in the treasure rumor," Judy mused.

"Bryce himself said it wasn't worth much, just sentimental value."

"He could have said that to throw us off. Did Bryce ever tell you how much he had?"

Hart's eyes sparked a hint of warning. *About what?* "He told me he panned for gold in Alaska and had only enough to fit in a small box."

"Which Louise promptly lost."

"When she was just a little girl." Hart's expression closed down, his eyes no longer inviting, obviously sticking up for his former neighbor. *Could I ever rate that much support?*

If Bryce had had that much faith in Louise, shouldn't she? Louise's will directed the fate of the farm. *Shouldn't I respect her wishes?* But what had Ardyth said about thinking Louise wanted to change her mind?

"Louise loved that place," Hart said. "Family and heritage meant everything to her. She even told me she hoped you'd come home more often. I never felt that growing up. I never knew any other family."

As Judy walked to the kitchen, for the first time the notion of being truly alone hit her. She'd never again have Christmas, or any other holiday for that matter, or share birthday gifts with a blood relative.

Judy reclaimed the basket that she'd used to carry the casserole. "I guess I'd better head home. Thanks again for sharing dinner with me."

Hart pushed open the door for her. Moths fluttered around the light above the screen door. "Thank you for bringing the casserole. If this makes you feel better, Louise was as content as she could be. She told me often that she was so glad she'd returned to the farm and wished she could have raised you here."

"I think I would have liked that," Judy said, her gaze lingering on the shadowy cleft below Hart's mouth. "I wish everything was different."

By the end of the week Judy felt frazzled, ready to declare her whole situation quits and return to Lewiston.

Graham had breezily checked in twice by phone for a total of seven minutes. He'd rambled nonstop the whole time and hadn't asked a thing about events in her life. What had she seen in him in the first place? She didn't bother to return his last message in which he'd asked again to come see her at the farm. Absence had not made her heart grow fonder. Who came up with such nonsense, anyway?

But she had to focus on the good. Hart had taught her about the chickens, and he promised a lesson on the tractor. He told her, too, what had been planted and the expected rotation of cutting and baling hay. Judy found an additional reason to respect her late aunt.

On the day of the meeting with Red and Gene Reynolds, she arrived at the lawyer's downtown office smack-dab on time.

"Come in, come in, Judy. Have a seat. Red will be along shortly." She and Reynolds spoke about Robertsville, the schools, and had started in on the government when Hobart hurtled in. Judy smelled the cut alfalfa left in the cuffs of his overalls. His dirty cap was twisted sideways on his grizzled head, and his fingernails showed grimy grease stains.

"Sorry. I'm sorry I'm late. Here, Judy." Hobart

thrust a rectangle of paper at her.

Judy took and opened a bank-issued check for five thousand dollars. She looked from breathless, sweaty Hobart to Reynolds's foxy grin. *Calculating. He wonders if this cash will lure me into wanting more.*

"Down payment on the rent I owe," Hobart blurted. He pulled off his cap and scrunched it in front of his overalls. "I'll make amends, Judy, I promise."

Judy looked up into his narrowed eyes. "Yes, but—"

"We'll have to talk later." Red slapped the dirty cap on his head. "Excuse me, but I have to git going. Appointment with the ag agent." He shuffled back through the door, the check and lingering odor the only indications he'd been in the room.

"I'm confused, Mr. Reynolds." Judy eyed her aunt's pudgy attorney. "Two days ago all he could talk about was when could he get the forty acres."

Reynolds leaned plump elbows on his desk as he measured her. "Apparently he's had a change of heart. A man should clear up his debts before moving on, I always say." He nodded at the paper in her hands. "That's yours. As Red said, a down payment on what he owes for back rent."

⚊

Judy swung her car into the driveway to see Clyde standing on the front porch. As she approached him, his grimace warned this was going to cost her money.

"Miss Judy, I fear I have bad news. Again." Clyde shook his brown-and-gray halo of hair, and she expected something to come flying out of it. "That new flooring? They sent the wrong thing entirely. Said another week before the right stuff comes in. I'm powerful sorry, ma'am."

Judy refused to allow her disappointment to overwhelm her. "Oh, well, Clyde, I guess we'll have to make do. Thank you for letting me know. The porch looks nice, though, with the new floorboards and rail. I appreciate it. Is there anything else we can do in the meantime?"

"Well, ma'am, now that you mention it, I did notice a *prob*lem wid the water heater. Unit's rusted."

"So what does that mean?" It seemed that Red's surprise rent payment would come in handy. Judy felt in her jeans pocket for the check. "We can't go without a water heater, now can we?"

Clyde cleared his throat and shifted uncomfortably.

"It's not your fault, Clyde." Judy ruefully agreed to the replacement of the heater and accepted Clyde's invitation to have lunch with his wife, Roxanne, the following week.

"Roxanne will be callin'."

"I look forward to meeting her."

Clyde clambered down the steps and into his van, and Judy stayed outside after he sputtered off. She'd just decided the grass tickling her ankles warranted a cutting when Ardyth pedaled in on her three-wheeled cycle.

"You're a welcome sight. You rescued me from lawn mowing." Judy smiled at her visitor. "I've got a pitcher of lemonade in the fridge."

"Sounds great," Ardyth said as she dismounted her bike.

A few minutes later, Ardyth set down her sweating aluminum cup on the porch step and leaned against the post. "I remember this set of glasses. Harold's mother bought them after the war when aluminum was all the rage. I loved to draw pictures with my finger when the condensation formed. The green's still my favorite."

Judy picked up her blue cup. "Lots of memories here for you, huh?"

Ardyth nodded. "Oh yes." Her smile looked faraway. "The same family farmed this land since they first got here in the mid 1850s. Raised tobacco in those days. Hard to imagine anyone but a Jamison living here. I loved coming to visit when I was growing up. I only had one older brother—and a sister who died at seventeen. My brother and my parents fought so much. But Harold's mother and father were nice folks. Restful."

"I never met them."

"Well, no, you wouldn't have, I guess. Let's see now. Rhoda, Harold's mother, was a Warner, from over in Edgars. They met at the county fair or something like that, if I recall. She died, um, before Louise was born, I know. And John passed on just after I moved away. Neither of them very old. That was the way of things back then, I guess. Poor Louise follows in the natural order. Harold and Una ran the farm by themselves practically since they were first married."

Judy felt a sudden chill and wrapped her arms around her midsection. "Family and traditions are pretty important."

"Yes, I guess they are." Ardyth picked up her cup again. "Mostly, times were just slower then. No one ever said that they didn't have enough time to help out. We knew when wash day came or weeding day, picking day or canning."

Judy settled back into the rocker. Ardyth could sure teach her students a thing or two about history. "What about winter?"

"We spent time at our schoolwork, I suppose. We had a lot of memory work. I recall doing recitations to anybody who sat still long enough to listen. My poor oma—I think she learned better English in the last five years of her life than all the time before."

"Your family emigrated? From where?"

"That wasn't so uncommon, you know. Even your family did, at one time. My oma and opa came from Germany, long before the war. You probably teach about that in your class."

"Yes, I do. Most of the kids are far removed from their roots. Hearing you talk about it makes it real. I love to get speakers in for the lessons, but you can probably figure out that, as time passes, there are fewer people who have known a different lifestyle."

"My, that's sad," Ardyth said. She abruptly changed subjects. "So, tell me about yourself."

Judy blinked and cleared her throat. "Oh, I'm not terribly exciting. I lived with Aunt Louise, you know. She raised me to be a good girl, to go to church and prayer meetings and youth groups and summer mission trips for Bible school and babysit. I sang in the girls' choir and was in the Future Teachers' Club. Then

I went to college, and now I teach school."

Judy felt Ardyth's little black eyes, steady and kind, fixated on her while she spoke. She relaxed enough to be able to talk about Louise.

"I miss her. . .my aunt. I barely remember my own mother and father. I don't even think about them much. But as much as I want to keep this house and land in the Jamison family, I don't think I'm brave enough to give up everything I know for a new life in Robertsville."

Ardyth brought her cool hand over Judy's entwined fingers.

"Oh, there, now. You might surprise yourself. Louise always had a good head on her shoulders, even as a little girl in my Sunday school class. I knew she had a deep faith, the kind that didn't need to question too much but somehow knew the truth from a lie. Appears she raised you proper." Ardyth's face crinkled in a pleasant smile. "You'll be fine. Everything turns out the way it's supposed to in the end, if you just have enough faith." Her bird mouth puckered while she peered off in the distance at the few walnut-sized apples hanging from the tree across the yard.

She and Ardyth sat in companionable silence looking out on the orchard, each with her memories. Judy's gaze settled on the oak stump.

"Say, Ardyth, you don't know anything about that stump out there, do you? Letters are carved on it, only I can't read them."

"Of course I do, dear. That picture I showed you, the one in the front parlor—that's the tree."

"Really? The one with the swing?"

"The very one. Struck by lightning. Took a long time to die. The boys used to have a fort up there. They always let me in. I was about the only girl who could climb the rope, anyway." Ardyth tilted her chin, looking proud of her feat. "That summer before we graduated, I remember Harold being in a funk about whether or not to finish high school, while his father made a huge stink that he had to. My, what a hullabaloo. Harold's father put it like this: 'It's winter, anyway. We don't need you so much, so you might as well improve your mind.' Of course, when old Joe came home before Christmas that year, he changed everything with his stories. You can imagine the journey from Alaska through the mountains in all the snow. Like straight out of the movies. He showed off those shiny flakes of gold of his and filled the head of every boy and girl around here with dreams of riches. Only Harold and Bryce—they did more than dream. That's all they talked about. Made me sick."

Ardyth clunked her cup on the porch floor. "Well, anyway, water under the bridge. So you can still see those letters carved in the tree strump? Looks like hearts?"

Ardyth might be on in years, but her indignant demeanor matched that of the teens Judy taught. "Yes," she said, holding back a chuckle.

"Let's go look!" Ardyth rocked to her feet, and they hiked over to the remains of the once-mighty oak.

Ardyth circled the tree stump first. "We had so much fun. We climbed; we made forts. We swung from the branches. Once I even collected acorns and planted them to make an oak tree farm. Nothing happened, of course. The squirrels cleaned up after me."

Judy soaked in her friend's childhood memories with relish.

Ardyth leaned in. "Yes, I remember this very well. Bryce came up with the idea the summer we graduated." She beckoned. "Come look. They didn't tell me what they'd done at first. I had to find out later." The lines about her mouth showed white. Judy saw for the first time the mottled brown patches of aged skin on her wrinkled neck. Ardyth's unchecked irritation aged her.

"You can recognize *H* for Harold. This side, there's the *B* for Bryce, of course. In the middle is my name. Genevieve Ardyth Anderson. *G A A*. Doesn't that look . . .twisted?" Ardyth clucked her tongue. "I'll tell you, I was never so humiliated in all my life. Those two Cretans!" She straightened, and tears reddened her eyes.

"I'm sorry, Ardyth. I didn't mean to make you feel bad. You don't have to say any more."

"Oh, I will. I want you to know. Not just because I'm still so mad after all this time, or have hard feelings for. . .Bryce. Maybe I should have been flattered. But when you're young, you just don't always see things for what they are." She paced into the first row of the orchard. "Before Bryce and Harold left for Alaska, they made a bet."

"Yes, Bryce told me that."

Ardyth's eyes narrowed. "So, he admitted it?"

"Well, yes. Just that he—well, he and Uncle Harold were—um. . ."

"Yes, yes," Ardyth said. "Humph. Una told me later. Imagine! 'Whoever pans the most gold gets the girl.' The most vulgar, medieval thing I ever heard. I never wanted anything more to do with either of them after that." She hugged herself, her lips a hard, grim line.

Judy wondered at the strength of Ardyth's hurt after all these years. Ardyth continued to talk.

"I kept in touch with Harold and Una, you know, after I moved away and married my Tom. Christmas cards and photos of the kids. Several years later Harold wrote that Bryce lost that gold of his, much to my delight. That makes me sound like a mean and bitter old woman, I know, but that's how I still feel about it."

—

The new toilet arrived. Judy went out to the orchard to get away from the plaster dust and the hiss and heat of the blowtorch Chet wielded with silent abandon. She couldn't study in that racket, and she would rather be in the fresh air anyway. She amused herself by thinking of words beginning with *P*. A porcelain pot planted just outside the back door in preparation for going potty while reading a periodical. She giggled all the way across the yard. Maybe she should keep the pre-used one, plant pansies in the bowl, or some other purpose.

Today seemed as good as any to look for the bomb shelter. Since she couldn't see anything above ground that indicated a location, she stopped at the garage to grab a spade and a sturdy spike.

An hour later, Judy wiped a hand across her moist forehead and tied her hair up in a loose ponytail. She looked back to where she'd finally left a metal bar stuck in the ground for a marker. Art's directions had been vague at best. "Twenty yards this side of the big apple tree." Fifty years later, it was kind of hard to tell where exactly "this side" started. Judy made an educated guess about the tree, which by all rights should have been chopped down or replaced long ago. Fruit trees didn't have long careers. She poked the rod into the ground at intervals, pleased that she could force it over half a foot. Just how deep did they cover the thing, anyway?

Judy rammed the pole as deep as she could. She reclined on the grass, staring up at the sky, and found a Carranza-shaped cloud. While she contemplated her next move, the Carranza-cloud appeared to stretch and pounce before dissipating. Judy sat up when she realized that the remodeling noises at her house had ceased.

Clyde and his nephew waved to her and drove off in the truck. Must be lunchtime. Judy ventured into the kitchen, pleased that the whole place wasn't covered in dust. Clyde had rigged plastic sheeting and swept up before leaving. He and Chet returned twenty minutes later.

After a quick sandwich, Judy went back to the orchard and dug two rows of pits about twelve inches deep at three-foot intervals before being interrupted.

"Whoa! What's going on here? Need a new septic system?"

Judy, who'd been in the process of throwing a shovelful of dirt, shrieked and tossed the shovel with the load. Heart pounding, she closed her eyes and took a deep breath. Hart leaned against a tree, laughing. "I'm sorry. You either must have been really concentrating or in another world. I didn't mean to scare you."

"Yeah, well, if you gave me a gray hair, I'll sock you," Judy said and sank to her knees.

"Are you okay?" Hart came to crouch next to her.

Judy shook her ponytail off of her neck. "Just not in as good of shape as I was this morning. You look like you're feeling more limber. Are the ribs better?" She wiped a hand across her forehead.

Hart gave a low whistle and helped her stand. "Yes. So what are you doing? Digging for treasure?"

"Ha, ha." She went to grab her shovel.

Hart followed. "Are you looking for the bomb shelter?"

Judy stopped. "If the shelter's deteriorated, it could pose a liability if I sell." She indicated the house, from which banging sounds emanated again. "Since Clyde's busy in there, I just thought I'd poke around out here."

"Literally. You know, there's an easier way."

"Oh? Art told me what he remembered."

Hart snorted. "What? From fifty years ago or something?"

"Well, yes."

"You could just go check with the county clerk. Harold had to have gotten some kind of permit, don't you think? The county would have a record, probably, including the building site on the property."

"Oh. I wouldn't have known that."

They both watched a lumberyard delivery truck come in.

"Looks like they'll start drywalling," Hart noted. "You're giving the house a nice makeover. Well done."

Judy felt herself flush at his openly frank appraisal. What should she say? She looked away. The moss-covered tree stump caught her eye. "Harold and Bryce carved their initials in that tree when they were kids. Would you like to see?"

"Sure." Hart shouldered the shovel while they walked. Judy put a hand up to her hair, feeling stray strands blowing around her ears. She released the band that held it back and ran her fingers through the snarls. Hart set the shovel down when they reached the oak.

"This must have been a grand old oak. See how thick the bark is?"

Judy knelt, shunting aside tall grass. "Here. This is the place." She trailed her fingers in the moss.

Hart joined her. He rubbed at the green growth then reached for his pocketknife. With a glance at her for permission, he carefully dug away some of the softer plant material. They stared at the faded design, three hearts interlocking.

Hart rubbed his finger over the letter of the heart on the left. "I'm guessing that's an *H* for Harold. And Bryce, here. What's the *G*?"

"Ardyth's first name is really Genevieve," Judy said.

Hart picked at the indentation on the right. "They must have been childhood sweethearts. But who went with whom?"

"That's another story. Ardyth told me about it earlier. Not Uncle Harold, but—"

Judy heard Clyde calling her name and got to her feet. He stood outside the back door with Chet, waving. He stopped when he saw he had her attention. The men began to pack up their equipment.

Judy smiled at Hart. "Looks like Clyde's on his way out for the day. I didn't realize it was so late."

Hart rose, too. "I plan to return your casserole dish. But my mother also taught me to never to return a dish empty, so I wonder if you'd like to come over again sometime. For supper."

Judy ducked her chin and reached for the shovel. She looked uncertainly at her house then back at the stump. Her thoughts raced faster than she could catch up and examine them. *Was this a date? What about Graham?* She squinted up at Hart's dark head, haloed in the late afternoon sun. She tried to conjure a picture of Graham. The image came too slow.

"Thank you. I think that would be nice. Eating alone isn't always so pleasant."

Hart nodded. "I'll call you then. I just want to check things out here before I go home."

Judy watched his every step to the barn. She grimaced in self-ridicule as she walked through the mudroom. At least she managed to keep her foot out of her mouth that long.

The answering machine blinked for attention. Judy snapped down the button. Chief Hutchinson's recorded voice announced that he'd received the toxicology report.

9

Chief Barry Hutchinson appeared to be listening intently into the phone at his desk when Judy walked into Robertsville's police station the next morning. The chief had only four other officers working for him, and two of those were part-time weekend help. He motioned for Judy to help herself from the carafe of viscid black liquid and then pointed to a chair near his rectangular slab of a workstation.

Judy politely declined the coffee and seated herself. She set her purse on the floor and composed herself to hear bad news. The man's desk held a surprising array of photographs in frames and two healthy philodendrons in gold pots. Barry made faces at the phone, as if to hurry the call, and exaggerated a yawn for her benefit. Judy nodded and returned his smile to let him know she understood the situation. She couldn't help notice the papers under his forearm, though, wondering if one of them was the report.

"Thank you. Yes, I will look into that. Yes. Thank you for calling. I have someone waiting. No, that's all right. Good-bye, Mrs. Birdseye."

Barry made a mock sweeping gesture across his forehead after he hung up. "I'm so sorry."

"I understand. You said you have the report? What does it say? What caused Aunt Louise's death?" She couldn't seem to stop the tumble of words.

Barry's hunched-over position and the twitch of

his nose told her of the man's disappointment louder than if he'd shouted the news. "Judy, I'm afraid the report doesn't give us any further insight."

"Wh–what do you mean, Chief?"

The phone rang. Hutchinson ignored the summons. He held up the pages of the pitifully short report and studied them. She wasn't fooled by his pretense, for his hands shook. "It says here that no toxic substances were found in Louise's system. None of the tests revealed anything. Not even an aspirin."

"You're sure? No poison? How can that be? But the coroner said she had classic signs of poisoning."

"I know, and you're right. And if there was foul play, like I suspect, I'm as eager as you are to catch the culprit." Chief wagged his head. "But I called the lab myself before I left you a message. I just couldn't believe it."

"So, they're sure there's no mix-up? Maybe this is someone else's report by mistake. You know—"

"I know. Those kinds of things happen, but I talked to the coroner myself. He said he didn't understand. Something had to have caused the massive hemorrhaging that poor Louise. . .ah, nothing about this makes sense."

Hutchinson threw the page down and leaned back, making the chair squeal in protest. He wouldn't meet her eyes.

Judy reached for the report and flipped open the file. Most of the language was incomprehensible but for the bottom line. She forced herself to look at the accompanying graphic photographs showing the hemorrhages under Aunt Louise's skin. *Rationalize. Analyze.* "If Louise wasn't poisoned, what else could cause this kind of damage?"

Hutchinson's expression turned brooding. "The crime lab is so backed up, I haven't been able to get anyone to talk to me. The coroner just flat-out said he didn't know. I called Bradshaw, the doc on call at RCH, and he said he'd do some research when he had time. He told me that some substances are hard to test for unless you have just the right equipment. There's even some poisons that don't show up at all if too much time has passed before they do tests."

Judy nodded. "I understand. Do you think I could talk to Dr. Bradshaw myself?"

"Definitely." Hutchinson wrote a number on a slip of paper and passed it to her.

"And I do appreciate your efforts, Chief."

Little Robertsville Community Hospital might have nice doctors who'd do some research, but if she wanted answers right away, she'd have to find them elsewhere. Unfortunately, Internet service providers were slow and few between in this part of the country. Judy's hookup left her frustrated, and her e-mail accounts had yet to import into her computer. Using the Internet for research might be as slow as RCH. What about the library?

"Chief, do you know anyone else we can try? Or do you have any other connections around the state or even out of state, maybe a university professor who specializes in this sort of thing?"

"What are you asking? Assassination without a trace?"

Hutchinson shook his head. "That kind of thing doesn't happen in Robertsville."

Judy leaned forward over the chief's desk. "Barry, you know as well as I do that those KOWPIE people are behind this." She stabbed at the file with her forefinger. "Aunt Louise didn't die naturally; that's obvious to anyone who sees these photos."

Barry's brows drew close. "I've told you what I know about those people. You stay out of it. Let us take care of them. There's no hint of poison in Louise's blood or tissues, and we have to respect the report. I'm sorry."

Judy felt her lips tighten in despair and stared at the impersonal manila folder. "Can't we get another opinion?"

"On an autopsy? We'd have to disinter the body. Do you know how much that would cost?"

Judy shook her head, a plan forming in her mind. If the chief refused to help any other way, she'd get to the bottom of her aunt's death herself.

"We may never understand why your aunt died the way she did, but you're going to have to let this go. For now."

Judy glanced up quickly to catch the faintest glimmer of hope under those bushy brows. She nodded at him to show him she understood his unspoken determination to learn the truth about Louise's death. No matter what the record showed.

～

As Judy turned off the rural road, she noticed the little blue car in her driveway. Anger spiked. What was

Graham doing here? Uninvited?

Standing on the lawn in front of her house, her erstwhile boyfriend held out his arms to her. "Judy! Babe! You didn't return my calls. I had to see if you were all right."

Out of the corner of her eye, Judy noticed Carranza beginning to slink along the front porch railing with the same look in his eye that she'd seen when he hunted cowbirds.

"Graham." She kept her distance, putting out a hand to ward him off when he reached out to hug her. "I wasn't expecting you. What can I do for you?"

"Ouch! Babe, that's cold. Is that any way to greet your fiancé?"

Judy focused on a point just behind Graham's head where Carranza came to a halt. The cat's tail began to twitch. She moved past Graham, trying to draw him away from the porch railing. Instead, Graham appeared rooted to the spot. He folded his arms and twisted his hips to keep her in sight.

Should she warn him about Carranza's occasional lapse in judgment and tendency to pounce? "Fiancé? We haven't talked about marriage, Graham. I'm even debating whether or not to return to Lewiston. In fact, I'm looking into other work. We only dated a couple of months, and not even exclusively."

"Hey. I never dated—well, just once. Or twice. But those were country club functions and you weren't available. What was I supposed to do? Come on, Judy. I put a lot of time and effort into this relationship. I came out here trying to make nice. I know how much you want to stay out here, and I do, too. . . . Owww!"

Judy watched dispassionately as Carranza flew through the air with the greatest of ease and landed, claws fully extended, on Graham's back.

"Judeeee!"

Judy managed to pull the cat off the twirling Graham. Carranza immediately went limp and slipped out of her grasp. He charged a few body lengths away and turned and looked at them both through haughty eyes before he sat and began to repair his ruffled coat.

"Judy!" Graham spun around again, his face a mask of anger.

"Here, Graham. Stop that. Let me see." Judy ordered him to sit on the step of the porch while she went to find some lotion and bandages. She returned to find Graham hunched over.

Graham stared at her, his mouth pouty. "What's with that animal? Did you train it to be an attack cat or something?"

Judy motioned for him to pull his shirt off so she could look at the scratches. She knelt behind him to wipe at the bloody slashes. "Of course I didn't *train* Carranza to attack. He's got a mind of his own."

Graham reached back and grabbed her wrist, stopping her ministrations. "We need to get some things straightened out."

Judy leaned back on her knees and wrested her arm from his grip. "You're right. We do." She bit her lip. "I don't want to marry you." She looked at him in time to notice the dark color suffusing his cheeks, his widened pupils and flaring nostrils indicating anger.

"I'm sorry," she whispered. "A lot of girls like you. You shouldn't—"

"I don't want just any girl! I need. . .I want you." Graham heaved himself up abruptly, hauling the torn shirt back over his head. He stepped a few paces into the yard and waved an arm. "Look at all this, Judy. You can't live here alone. Take care of this land. You need someone to help you. Now, be reasonable." Carranza had not moved. Graham hesitated when his trajectory would have taken him near the cat. "Come back with me. If you do, we—we can hire someone to work the farm. Yeah. . .that might work. We'll live in Lewiston and come back here whenever we want. You've got a good job. You don't need to get another in this podunk town. And I can take care of us both if you don't want to teach anymore."

"Why did you really come here, Graham? What's so important about this farm that you needed to talk to Louise?" Judy stood, holding the bloody washcloth in both hands. "I don't understand. You're not a farmer, and this land isn't. . ." Judy closed her mouth. The land was valuable. Mr. Reynolds said so. But how would Graham know that? *Of course, anybody who reads the papers knows how valuable land is.*

Graham put his hands on his hips. He cut a faintly menacing figure, and Judy rubbed at goose bumps on her forearms. "Listen, Graham. Louise's will tied up this property. Unless I live here, I lose it." Graham didn't move. He stood in front of the setting afternoon sun. She couldn't read the expression on his face, but she no longer cared to. "I think you'd better leave, Graham.

Neither of us has anything to gain from pursuing a relationship. I don't want to see you anymore."

"Judy—"

Carranza let loose with his unearthly howl and pounced. They both turned to watch him shake a rodent of some kind. Graham started crunching across the gravel to his car. He faced her before getting in. "I don't think you know what you're doing. You're still grieving for that aunt of yours, but someday you'll come to your senses and realize you need me." He gave the grounds a sweeping, proprietary glance. "When things get out of control, you let me know. I'll be there for you."

Carranza growled deep in his throat. Graham hopped into his car and drove off, spitting stones in their direction.

Carranza trotted up to her, meowed, and dropped his prey at her feet. This time his offering, a little grey shrew, showed bloody foam about the mouth, its glassy eyes staring in pitiful supplication.

Clyde and Chet were scheduled to lay the new floor in the bathroom at the end of the week. Judy heaved a huge sigh of relief when Clyde approached to give his final report. She dug her checkbook out of her purse and looked expectantly at him for a bill.

Clyde rubbed his hands. "Chet, there, is jus' finishing the molding. You'll be able to walk on it right away. So, then, that's about all. Unless you'd like me to look at your roof."

"Oh? You think I should do something about it? How old do you think it is?"

As usual, Clyde looked repentant. "I did ask around, see if anybody recalled who did the work last. Trey at the hardware store got his dad, who thought old John Kronberg and his outfit did the work. Near about forty years ago is what they recall. At the end of life for those shingles. There's some sway to it that I don't like to see. I really think we ought to go up in the attic and check things out."

"I guess it wouldn't hurt. Do you want to do that now?"

"Yes, ma'am."

Judy led the way to the pull-down ladder in the middle of the wide second-story hallway. "I haven't been up here in ages," she chattered to cover her trepidation over going into unfamiliar and potentially scary territory.

The trapdoor proved to open easily. Judy climbed through into the large, airy room that held the scent of aged wood. Dust sheets draped intriguing heaps of mysterious items. One small round window let in late afternoon light. The usual debris of generations—fraying trunks, stacks of yellowed newspapers, canning jars, and LPs—lined the outer edges of the room. She and Clyde stepped gingerly across rafters, looking down to watch their footing, and then upward to examine the underside of the roof. He shone a silver torch along the exposed rafters.

The one shape she thought she recognized under

the eaves had to be Aunt Louise's wooden dollhouse. Judy had been allowed to play with the beautiful house and the tiny resident family, the Porters, on her scant visits. She promised herself that she'd come back up later and look at it.

"Well, ma'am, I would recommend a complete tear off. See, here." Clyde flashed the light along the seams of warping plywood. "The deterioration? It would be in your best interest to go ahead and redo the whole kit 'n caboodle." He flicked the button off so they were in shadow.

Judy followed him back downstairs, pulling the trapdoor closed behind her. "What do you say, Clyde? Do colored shingles cost more? I wondered if blue would look nice, if I ever had to do this. And I also read about a new style of metal."

They came to an agreement whereby Clyde would return in a few weeks after a short job he had on his schedule. "And by the way, I only make use o' green materials in my work," the contractor told her. Chet joined him as they prepared to leave.

"Green?"

"Yes, ma'am. Recycled and the like."

"Oh. That's great. Anything to save the environment." Judy gave him a thumbs-up.

Clyde's expression through the thick glasses sobered with fierce concentration. "The earth is our greatest con*cern*. Without it, there would be no 'us.' "

A sudden thought flashed in her mind. "Clyde, what do you know about KOWPIE?"

His coke bottle lenses caught a stray reflection of

the lowering sun. "Cow pie, ma'am? Seems you got plenty around here. Now, I heard some folks use 'em for furnace fuel. I can look into it for you—"

"No, no. The organization." She hoped he wouldn't lie, for she didn't know how to tell him that someone else had already informed her about his activities.

Clyde hung his head. "Well, ma'am, I hoped you didn't mean them folk. I'm ashamed to tell you that for a while the missus and me bought into their way of thinking. Until we saw the guns and the like. We got scared and backed right out. We've never held with violence. No way." He shook his head for emphasis.

Judy stared at him thoughtfully, relieved she didn't have to reveal the source of her questioning. "Do you know anyone I could speak to with the. . .what do you really call yourselves? Surely not cow pies?"

Clyde threw his head back and guffawed. "Nah. Nothing like that. Called ourselves Woodsmen, actually. But I'm not sorry to say that me and Roxanne left that bunch and hightailed it to Robertsville. Set up my business, been happy ever since. Got family here."

Chet raised his beefy head and almost smiled before once again studying the laces on his huge steel-toed boots.

"And I'm not sorry to say I do not keep in touch with anyone from that mess. Not even a Christmas card. Why do you want to find them, anyhow? Nothing but criminals, if you ask me. Best to keep away from 'em." Clyde tossed his toolbox into the van. "Well, I'd best go place the order for the new roof."

He and the silent Chet finished packing up their

equipment. Judy handed him a check for his work so far and a down payment on the roofing materials. Chet thanked her, and they drove off in the faded work van.

If only he'd been able to help put her in touch with a member of KOWPIE. There had to be someone who knew about the deal with the farm. At least Clyde confirmed Reynolds's story. But how could she prove Ardyth's theory that Louise had wanted to change her will after all?

10

After parking in the town square lot, Judy stood outside her car for a moment deciding which way to go. Should she track down permits and records for the bomb shelter or go grocery shopping first?

"Judy! Judy Winters!"

She whipped her head around. Laura Reynolds was across the street, waving and calling her name. "Gene would like to talk to you if you have a minute!"

Judy waved back and sauntered over.

"I'm glad you came in, Judy," Reynolds said, after ushering her into his office and showing her a seat. "I missed you at home."

"What did you want to see me about, Mr. Reynolds?"

"Call me Gene, please." He walked around his desk and picked up a folder. "Country Properties has made a firm offer," he said. "Here's the contract. We've got three days to look it over and perhaps counter. I think the amount is generous and fair. And it doesn't take into account the fact that the local government might not grant the subdivision rights at this time." He sat down. "Which is a major point in your favor."

Judy scanned the documents. Considering that the Reynoldses owned the company, she was surprised the man continued to speak of Country Properties as some third-party entity. She crossed her legs and began bobbing her toe then looked at the number on the bottom line and back up at the agent. Reynolds smiled from ear to ear.

"Um, wow, I guess."

Reynolds stopped smiling and leaned against his desk, his arms crossed. "I'm getting the feeling that you're not as enthused about this as I am."

"I'm stunned. I don't know what to say. And how can you get around Louise's last wishes in her will?"

"I did mention an offer of this magnitude to you when you first arrived. Along with the fact that once you took ownership, you could certainly hire a manager for the next few years. The will didn't stipulate what kind of farming you had to do or that you couldn't sell some of the acreage."

"Oh." Judy gripped the several-paged contract in both hands. "You did. I remember. So much has happened since then." She flipped through the pages again. "Where would I find a manager, anyway?"

Reynolds smiled and folded his chubby little hands in front of him. "Why, I could certainly help you there, young lady."

"I thought I might stay here all summer." Judy stopped to examine a clause in the contract. "So you might tear down the house?"

Reynolds shifted in his seat. "Well, that's the way the paragraph could be interpreted."

"But I'm fixing it up now."

The agent's new expression was not so genial. He pulled the black glasses off with one sweeping gesture. "You can counter. Of course, if you wanted to, you could keep the house and buildings or an acre or something. That would change the price, of course."

"Oh, I could? That's something to think about."
Judy stood. "So, I've got a couple of days to think
about this, right?"

Reynolds followed as she left the office. "When
you do make a decision, please let me know right away.
Counter offers take some consideration."

"Okay, I will. I was just going to City Hall to check
whether they had records that might shed some light as
to where Uncle Harold put the bomb shelter."

"Yes. It would be good to get that straightened
out. We can fill in the shelter. Prevent liability."

Judy stopped at Laura's desk. Laura looked up
at them, her baby blue eyes wide and innocent. She
nodded as if she'd been part of their conversation.
"That's a good idea." She appeared to read her husband's
expression. "That's a sweet offer by Country," she said.
"You won't get another like that soon from anyone
else."

"Thank you." Judy glanced from one to the other.
Something was very odd about the way they referred to
their own business. "Good-bye."

Judy stared at the contract again after she took it
to her car. *Okay, what's wrong with me? This is a great
offer. Why am I even hesitating?*

Judy's lunch with Roxanne, Clyde's wife, posed an
intriguing possibility. Roxanne worked in the school
district office and told Judy that a short-term contract
to cover a maternity leave for one of the two fifth-
grade teachers for the next school year would soon be
posted. If she was interested and could round up her

papers, licenses, and references, Roxanne would set up an interview. The lunch included an impromptu tour of the school campus and a favorable meeting with the administrator and elementary school principal.

Judy had indeed been interested. Returning to Lewiston no longer held the same appeal as it had in June. Maybe Robertsville was meant to be her home. But if she lived on the farm, would she suffer the same fate as Louise?

She locked her car this time and went to the county records office to search for information on Harold's bomb shelter. A woman perhaps ten years older than Judy answered her query at the department's front desk. "Sure, we can try to find that for you. You don't have the exact date, do you?"

"No, I'm afraid not."

"Well, we can look up in the computer what kind of permits were issued for what property. What's the legal description?"

Fortunately, she was prepared for that question and gave her the range and section number.

"Yes, here we are." The woman glanced up at her from the computer screen. "Not too many bomb shelters around here. That was before my time. I'll just get you a copy of the permit, then. It gives measurements from the existing structures. That should help. If your people followed the directions, that is. That'll be a dollar and seventy-five cents."

Judy added the copy of the permit to the pile of papers in her car and drove to the market.

"This is getting to be a nice happenstance," Ardyth

greeted Judy in the parking lot. The older woman was settling a bag in the wire basket of her three-wheeled cycle. "Let me return the favor and have you over for lemonade this time. Please."

"Why, thank you. I wanted to talk to you more about Aunt Louise anyway—and ask your opinion about an offer I'm considering."

"Mmm, my. I don't know how good I am at offering advice. But I can listen. And if you need to buy perishables, you can keep them in my refrigerator. I'm at 314 Maple Street, the little yellow bungalow."

"Gee, thanks," Judy said. "See you in a bit, then."

Ardyth waved before she pedaled away.

A half hour later, Judy handed Ardyth her bag with yogurt and butter to keep cool in her refrigerator.

"You'll have to be the one to remember it, dear, when you leave."

Judy smiled. "I'll try," she promised.

The older woman waved at the back screened-in porch. Judy could see wicker furniture and plants through the open door. "Go on in and make yourself at home. I'll be right there."

"Yes, thanks." Judy examined photographs of those who were obviously family members. She had just picked up an ornately framed photo of a young man when Ardyth came in with a round tray of glasses of lemonade and slices of coffee cake.

"Here we are. Ah, I see you have Paul in your hands." Ardyth stepped around a marmalade cat stretched out in a pool of sun to get to Judy's side. "Spitting image of his father, isn't he? My oldest. Come, sit."

Ardyth settled herself on a bright cushion. She picked up her glass and urged Judy to do the same.

"Oh, this is fresh," Judy said. "You used real lemons?"

Her hostess cocked her head. "Well, yes, that is how lemonade is made."

Judy stared at the pulp mingling with the ice cubes in her glass. "I usually open a can of frozen. I didn't know what I was missing. You'll have to show me how sometime."

"Of course, dear. That must mean you'd like to stay here in our little village."

Judy bobbed her head at Ardyth's prosaic comment. Her hostess rushed on. "Tell me about the remodeling."

She took the next ten minutes to explain about the new bathroom and the new roof. Then she turned the subject. "So, Ardyth, you moved to St. Louis, you said? And got married? How many children do you have?"

"Oh yes, I did. I was offered a good job and chance to have my own adventure. And I found a good man who wanted to be my husband. And so we had our family. There's Paul, my firstborn. He's an accountant, like his father. He's married and has two boys of his own. Bryan and Heath, both in high school. Then there's Robert, and my daughter, Gwen. Robert's married, too, with no children, and Gwen's just divorced. She's got my only granddaughter so far, Evaline. Evvie's nine. Stubborn little soul, with rippling brown waves of hair and eyelashes that make a breeze if you stand too close when she wants something from you."

"And Bryan's the one who visited here."

"That's right. He and your Carranza got along fine. He was so disappointed not to find the treasure before he had to get back home and go to work. He's a lifeguard."

Ardyth's cat came to mew and rub against her mistress's shins. "Old Cat, you can't be hungry already, are you?" Ardyth excused herself. "I'll just be a minute."

At the mention of her friend Carranza's name, Judy thought she saw Cat's ears perk. Cat lifted a paw to Judy, almost in supplication. Judy laughed. "Did you hear us talk about your boyfriend? Go along with Ardyth, now. She'll find you something to eat."

Cat's tail stuck straight up in the air as she pounced along after Ardyth. Judy went to explore the spicy scent that seemed to come in waves in the bright sunroom. A green plant with trailing vines boasted frilly lavender flowers. Nothing in her porch looked like Aunt Louise's strange plant in the dining room at home.

When her hostess returned, Judy said, "For a while, I tried to think of a plan to have you keep Carranza. I don't think he was happy to see me."

"Oh? Louise loved having that cat around. As good as any guard dog, Louise would say."

Judy agreed and told her about the incident with Graham.

"Well, I'd trust Carranza's good taste. But I'm sorry things didn't work out with that young man. Perhaps you'll find someone else, now that you'll be staying on with us."

How could Ardyth know anything about her plans? Judy examined the woman's bright countenance suspiciously.

Ardyth chuckled. "Oh, I ran into Robin Grayson

after I left you. She teaches second grade and goes to Peace Church with us."

"Oh, I think I remember meeting her. She's nice. Young, right? Husband's a police officer? And she'd already heard that I applied to teach?"

"That's right. News in a small town like this spreads like ivy. See, I told you you'd fit right in."

Judy sipped the lemonade. The idea of fitting in pleased her. Ardyth's comment on her staying in Robertsville took care of one of the questions she'd wanted to ask. "Don't you miss your family?" As soon as she said that, Judy put her hand over her mouth. "Oh, I'm so sorry. That's none of my business. I don't know why I said that. Forgive me."

Ardyth chuckled. "I don't mind talking about it. Here, have some cake. And if you're considering relocation, I'd say it was a fair question."

Judy made herself comfortable in the wicker rocker while Ardyth lounged on her couch. Cat soon returned and jumped up beside her mistress. "I enjoyed the time I had with Tom, my husband, and of course the children. The boys and Gwen are very good about calling. And I get along fine with my daughters-in-law. We talk all the time. We visit. Tom was fifteen years older than me. He passed away nearly twenty years ago, already, just after our anniversary that year. Paul was a senior in high school." Ardyth stroked the cat. "Tom was a nice man."

Judy waited. A fly buzzed against the window.

"My best friend Ginny died last year. At Thanksgiving time." Ardyth continued to stroke Cat, who purred loudly and turned on her side, stretching paws in delicious luxury. "I just didn't think we were that old until I read her obituary. Ginny was a year younger than me. I love my family. But when the people you love start dying around you. . .it puts a different perspective on things."

By the taut lines around Ardyth's mouth and her slumped posture, Judy could see that the woman was struggling with this truth.

Ardyth swallowed a couple of times then shook her head. "I just didn't want to be the last one down there of all our friends, alive, alone, and needing to be taken care of. So I came home to my old friends, my old neighborhood."

"Bryce was one of your friends."

"Humph." Ardyth took a swig to finish her lemonade and set the glass on the end table with a *thump*. "Bryce Edwards. Humph. I've been back seven months and not once has he contacted me personally."

Judy gnawed her bottom lip to keep from grinning. "I have his telephone number, if you'd like to copy it."

Ardyth's frown lengthened. She absently rubbed Cat's ruff so hard that the animal's ears went back and she slithered off Ardyth's lap.

The ides of August gained rapidly. The sheriff closed Louise's case, but Judy wasn't satisfied. She felt justified in keeping the farm and decided that the least she could do for Louise was vindicate her death. Even Barry Hutchinson had moved on to other business.

Judy read in the newspaper that the militant

KOWPIE group had staged three noisy, disruptive protests about keeping the woods and lakes free from human intervention in northern Wisconsin that summer. They gained no sympathy by frightening away the tourist trade and upsetting those who relied on summer fare.

In the meantime, Judy continued to spruce up the house and sort through her late aunt's belongings. Once she'd worked through her initial grief, pleasant details of their life together seeped back into her memory. When they'd lived in Lewiston, Aunt Louise had kept track of the weather and made a daily report on their little garden in a series of journals. Louise also noted the visiting birds and the top news stories of the week. Judy longed to find Louise's journals. Perhaps they would shed light on the reasons her aunt had made such a deal with a militant organization. . .and maybe if she'd finally decided to change her mind. Judy disposed of clothing and personal items but couldn't find any trace of Louise's diaries.

Did Ardyth tell the truth about Louise changing her mind? No one else seemed to know about it. And what if Ardyth really did blame Louise for all those years of lost treasure? Surely Ardyth would have stayed and married Bryce if he'd had anything to offer her. Poison didn't need a strong man to administer. Especially if a low dose wouldn't register on an autopsy later.

Come on, Judy, this is Ardyth you're talking about. But how well do you know her? Not well at all.

11

Hart called to invite Judy over for supper as he had promised. She wondered if she should tell him about her breakup with Graham. She wouldn't bring up the subject out of the blue, she told herself, after contemplating several scenarios. Hart was only being polite, neighborly. He probably wouldn't ever be interested in someone like her, not raised on a farm or knowing anything about farm life. And her personal life shouldn't be any of his concern, anyway. Should it?

After their meal, Hart brought cups of coffee into the living room and placed one in front of her. "You're quiet."

"Thank you, Hart. I just have a lot on my mind, I guess."

"Anything I can do?"

Judy smiled at him. "Nice of you to offer, but I don't think so." Should she tell him about Graham now? She settled back on the couch, curling her legs underneath. "Bryce tells me that your family is up north, running a large farming operation."

Hart sat across from her in a new bentwood rocker.

"That's right. My folks are not quite Bryce's age."

Judy watched him over the rim of her cup, took a sip, and cradled it on her lap.

"My two older brothers run the dairy and the crops separately. They have a pretty big setup."

"Why didn't you stay?"

Hart studied the coffee-table crates for a moment. "My nephew Bobby is only seven years younger than I am. He's got his whole life wrapped up around farming. Wins every 4-H award there is. He's president of the ag club at school. Probably has a bigger bank account than me, with all of his fair winnings." Hart rocked forward.

"I wanted to go to school. Machinery fascinated me." He shrugged and picked up his cup. "Not just fixing it, but how it worked. So I studied engineering. I started learning about how to make things run more efficiently. I want to find out if we can take machines to a higher level. The safety standards can always be improved. I met Bryce Edwards at a seminar."

"Grad school is expensive."

"Didn't you say you were working on your master's degree?"

"That's right." She told him about the information she had gathered on population centers and the food distribution.

Hart stared out the darkened window behind her.

Embarrassment washed over her. She smiled. "This is boring. I'm sorry."

Hart rested his sherry brown eyes on her. "Not at all, Judy. It's a fascinating problem to consider. I wish more people would understand the potential disaster of not caring for the earth."

"Okay," she said, but she had a feeling he was only being polite.

"I was paying attention. Really. But wait here a minute. I need to check something."

Judy sat, looking around the living room with its lone couch and the rocker which Hart so abruptly vacated. His few magazines had titles like *Machining World* and *Engineering Week*. Judy stood to stretch her legs. The kitchen door swung open on a squeaky hinge, giving her a start.

Hart strode back into the room. His eyes shone. "I've got to oil that door." He paused then frowned. "What's the matter?"

"Did you see anyone out there?"

Hart's expression sobered. "I thought I saw something moving. I just wanted to be sure the pens were latched or there wasn't a stray dog or coyote. Your chickens aren't that far away." He moved to stand in front of her. "What's wrong? You weren't afraid for big, strong me, now, were you?"

Judy rubbed her arms and laughed at his attempted levity. "Well, if a girl can crack your ribs. . ."

Hart laughed, too. "Hey, now, no fair. That was like getting hit by a ton of bricks."

Judy raised her eyebrows in mock severity. "I'll have you know that I weigh no more than half a ton of bricks."

Hart joined her on the couch this time. "Only when you're going seventy miles an hour."

Judy took a deep breath. "I'm sorry." She put a hand on his arm and just as quickly moved it away.

Hart grinned. "No need to be so skittish, Judy. Really, what's got you nervous?"

Now I tell him. "I broke up with Graham a few days ago." Once that little bit of information was out, she couldn't seem to stop chattering. "I'm thinking of relocating to Robertsville and keeping the farm, but I'm worried that whatever happened to Louise might happen to me, too."

Hart was quiet for so long that she started to rise to leave. "I'm sorry, Hart. I'm sorry. I had no right to—"

Hart took her hand to stop her momentum. "Whoa, wait. I'm glad you confided in me. You're upset, and I want to help."

Judy lowered herself to the cushion again. She searched his expression carefully. *Tight control. Why?* Did it bother him that she'd blathered on about her personal life?

Judy shook her head, unable to read him clearly. "Thanks. You've done so much already by helping us out—Louise and me, that is. I don't know why I even brought it up."

Hart's eyes opened slightly wider to indicate alarm. *Now what?* She hadn't been able to read the familiar little signs in him before. Why now? Everyone else around her read like an open book. What was she supposed to discover about Hart?

"Can we just talk some more, Judy?" Hart looked her directly in the eye. "What's got you so nervous? I promise, I'll do everything I can to make sure you'll be safe. I'm just a phone call away."

Judy found herself mesmerized by the gentleness of Hart's tone, the warmth of his hand surrounding hers.

"Tell me. . .tell me about staying in Robertsville. What about your job in Lewiston?" Hart's eyes never left hers. She found herself telling him about the temporary teaching position and then details of Louise's will and the Reynolds offer.

"So Reynolds's outfit wants to buy you out. Offered you a lot of money. And KOWPIE, hmm? They're the ones making all the fuss up north, right?"

"Yeah. Ardyth seemed to think that Louise wanted to change her will about leaving the farm to that organization if I didn't live there. If she did, she'd have written about it in her journal, I'm sure. Louise was fanatical about keeping a diary. I just haven't found them."

Hart abruptly changed tack. "Judy, do you mind if I ask about your folks? What happened to them?"

"They were killed in a train wreck when I was little."

"I'm sorry. That must have been terrible for you."

"I had just started first grade. Aunt Louise was so great. She moved in and took care of me. She was so determined to make her own way financially. She gave up almost everything for me. I feel. . .guilty, I guess, now that she had so little time back home on the farm with her father. I always knew she wanted to return. Louise never said that she hated living in Lewiston, but she did it for me. So that I'd be able to stay in a place I knew. She also tried to keep the memory of my parents alive. I was so young, though."

Hart nodded and squeezed her hand. "That had to be really tough on you."

Judy's eyes burned. She appreciated Hart's concern. Graham had never wanted to talk about his own background. He said he hadn't got on with his family and had bummed around the country before settling in Lewiston. She couldn't help comparing the differences between the two men. "Tell me something about yourself, Hart. How did you come to be renting Bryce's farm?"

Hart frowned just a second and looked up at the ceiling. "I just finished a semester of grad school. Things weren't going so hot in my personal life. I decided not to go into more debt for school and to take some time off. Bryce knew my situation and told me he had a place I could use for as long as I needed."

Hart got up to change the music they'd chosen after dinner. "Believe me, I had no intention of farming. I grew up on a farm and know firsthand how hard it is. Little place like Bryce's, you can hardly make enough to live on, let alone go to school. Three and a half years later, here I am."

"Why'd you stay?"

"I thought I'd take another year to raise cash. Corn prices started going back up. Soybeans, too. Bryce already had equipment he said I could use. I had time before I have to complete my degree. Louise came up with this plan for raising cattle. Said she hated to see the barn empty. I did some research, saw that I could make out all right, and we had ourselves a deal. My folks weren't that impressed. My dad and my brother Jim wanted to lend me money for school, but I didn't want to owe anyone."

"So it was just last year you and Louise started on the great moo adventure."

Hart laughed and sat back next to her, crossing

an ankle over his knee. "That's a good one. Yeah. I can expect a pretty good return if the market stays up."

"How much school do you have left?"

"Three semesters, if I go back soon. Otherwise, I'll have to start all over," Hart said.

"What did you mean, 'not so hot' in your personal life, if you don't mind my asking?"

"Fair's fair. I don't mind, I guess. There was a girl. We were supposed to get married. We'd started putting money down on the wedding and even looked at places to live." Hart picked up their coffee cups and headed toward the kitchen.

Judy followed. "I'm sorry I asked. I suppose it's none of my business."

"You told me about your boyfriend. I hardly think about Amber anymore."

Judy leaned a hip against the counter while he filled the sink with hot water and dish soap and set their dishes to soak. "Do you want some help?" He declined her offer. "Well then, I'd better get home," she said. She picked up her purse and pulled out her key ring in preparation to leave. "Thank you for a delicious meal. And the talk."

Hart accompanied her outside. "I'm glad you're sticking around, Judy Winters. I'd like to get to know you better." He opened her car door and gently clicked it shut after her. Judy had left the window open, and Hart leaned in toward her. "I want to help you figure out what happened to Louise, too. Don't hesitate to call if you need anything, okay? I'll be right there."

Would he kiss her? Before Judy could move toward

him, Hart backed away and waved.

Judy smiled at her foolish romantic notion and looked in the rearview mirror before backing out. She blinked when she thought she saw the bushes shiver. *Probably just a raccoon or something.*

No raccoon could make as much racket or shine lights intermittently as what woke Judy that night. She checked her bedside clock. *Three thirty! What in the world?* Judy crept along the wall to peek through the screen of her open bedroom window. Her room faced the backyard. She could barely make out a pickup truck sitting at the edge of the driveway. She squinted into the shadows and counted. One, two. . .three shadowy figures out there?

"Put that out!" A distinctively male voice whispered when a flashlight beamed across the grass. A moment later vehicle doors crashed shut, and the truck sped off.

Judy's heart thudded wildly. What were they looking for? She crept back to her nightstand and picked up the telephone. She realized she couldn't read the buttons and reached to turn on the lamp. Instead of finding the switch, she sent the lamp teetering on the edge of the stand. It crashed to the floor. Judy yelped and pulled her bare feet up onto the bed. With nerveless fingers, she pulled open the bedside drawer to reach for the tiny flashlight she kept there in case of power failure. In her fright, Judy pulled the drawer all the way out of the stand. Once she flipped the switch of the penlight, she dialed 911 and explained between gasps that she'd seen trespassers in her yard.

"No. . .I think they're gone," Judy replied to the operator's query.

The operator's calm voice assured her that a patrolling deputy would arrive shortly.

After disconnecting, Judy shone the light at the broken pieces of the ceramic lamp on the floor and then at the gaping slot in the nightstand. She clutched the shallow wooden drawer still on her lap, her ears tuned to every sound in the rickety house.

"Deep breaths," she whispered as she crawled to the foot of the bed and stepped gingerly around the sharp fragments. Pulling on a robe, she went to meet the officer, whose squad's strobe lights flashed through the window.

She and the young uniformed woman stood on the front porch while Judy described what she had seen from her bedroom window. The officer examined the yard and the gash of fresh tire tracks.

"I can't say if the tracks are from someone turning around or stopping to talk on a cell phone or even throwing out garbage. We get that a lot on the rural roads. You didn't get the make of the car or license plate or anything? You couldn't identify any of the people you say you saw?"

Feeling like she'd just awoken from a bad dream, she had no other choice but to agree with the deputy's assessment. "No, sorry, the entire thing was a blur."

"Tell you what. I've read the reports about Mrs. Jamison's accident."

Judy didn't correct the woman on "Mrs." to say

that her aunt had never married.

"You said you thought the trespassers were looking for something in the yard. Why don't I note in my log tonight a recommendation for someone to come around tomorrow to check the place over?"

"Thank you."

"You're welcome. You'll feel safer once you're back inside. You should always keep your door locked. Folks out here seem to have a hard time remembering that. We'll let you know if we hear anything. Good night." The officer flipped her notepad closed, got back into her vehicle, called in on the radio, and then drove off.

Too keyed up to sleep, Judy got out a broom and dustpan to sweep up the mess from the broken lamp. It looked old, and she hoped she hadn't accidentally destroyed a valuable antique. On her knees in front of the bedside table, she attempted to replace the drawer she'd pulled out earlier. When the drawer stuck, ramming it didn't seem to work.

Judy set the drawer down and got out the mini flashlight again. Aha! The bottom of the slide appeared to be warped. She put her hand inside to feel around. The board was loose, not warped, so she gave it another shake. No, not loose but completely free. She pulled the dusty wooden slat from the piece of furniture and sat back on her haunches, staring at the gaping dark place. The flashlight revealed a hidey hole.

Oh! A secret compartment. No wonder she hadn't found Louise's diaries earlier. Judy slowly drew out eight thin volumes and placed them beside her on the floor. She fingered the outside of the boxy night table.

She never considered that such a large hidden section took up the space under the drawer.

Judy recognized some of the five-year diaries from her childhood years and opened the pages to confirm the dates. Aunt Louise's spidery handwriting brought tears to her eyes. Clutching the last two books to her chest, she took them downstairs and curled up on the couch.

The older of the two books were dated about the time Judy finished college. Louise recorded temperature and news dutifully. Judy's graduation day had been partly cloudy and sixty-eight. Judy smiled. A year later, Louise noted that her father had suffered the first of two strokes.

"Fthr nds me mr than J," Louise wrote in her shorthand. "Mvng bck 2 farm @ last." The second stroke killed him shortly after. Judy paged through a half year's worth of crop notes, gentle complaints regarding Red's lack of rent payment, and lambastes against a community which apparently didn't have a clue that recycling would save the planet.

"Caut R. Harris thrwg prftly gd alm cn in grbg @ chrch," Louise wrote one Sunday. Judy smiled and yawned hugely. The words blurred until the shorthand became impossible to translate. Her eyelids met.

A heavy slam woke Judy. She blinked into bright sunshine and groaned. Her neck ached from falling asleep in an unnatural position against the back of the sofa. Who could be visiting today? She didn't expect company. She pushed aside the curtain at the kitchen window and saw Hart's truck parked near the barn.

Judy went to dress and check around her bedroom for more stray ceramic shards. She walked through the other bedrooms to round up another small lamp she could use in place of the broken one.

After a quick helping of toast and coffee, Judy went outside. Only eight thirty, the day was shaping into a scorcher. She replenished the water in the chicken pen. Hart had warned her that in the extraordinary heat and humidity, the chickens needed shade and plenty of water. Judy had taken to talking to them lately.

"Clucky, what would you do if you were me? I told that Mr. Reynolds I wanted another week at least to counter the Country offer. I'm afraid to give up my comfortable job in Lewiston for a temporary one in Robertsville. I like it here. Ardyth and Bryce have a complicated history with Louise. How much do I trust them? What if they were mad at Louise for losing the gold? People said they liked Louise, even if she annoyed them about their recycling habits. I could use Pastor Tyson for a sounding board, but it doesn't seem right since I'm not a member of the church. So that's why I'm out here, talking to chickens," Judy told her audience, through the round mesh of their enclosure. Clucky strutted over and nibbled mindlessly at the wire. The rooster bobbed its head up and down and suddenly made a diving thrust at the dirt. Hens cackled in the background.

Judy kicked at the dirt with her tennis shoe and

stared into the orchard. She should be praying to God instead of talking to the animals like some strange Dr. Doolittle. Maybe she could ask Hart to have lunch with her and pray, like at Bible study. The atmosphere felt oppressive. She held up a hand to shield her eyes. A haze settled where the orchard met the sky. No wonder Aunt Louise couldn't wait to return to the farm from Lewiston. Despite the heat today, the beautiful countryside was awesome.

Hart came around the side of the barn, driving the tractor. They waved at each other. Hart's offer to come if she needed him reverberated in her head. She had better tell him what she saw last night. They were neighbors. What if those people decided to continue their search on his property? At least he'd be warned. She wanted to tell him about Louise's diaries, too.

Judy admitted to herself that she couldn't stop thinking about Hart. He was in her thoughts wherever she went. She'd watched his every gesture as they sat at his kitchen table, eating dinner. She could still feel the touch of his hand on hers, see his brown eyes warm with depth of feeling as he told her about working with Louise.

Judy stared after the tractor. Hart parked in the barn. A dust devil blew up and just as quickly died down. She looked up at the sky. The haze on the horizon had mushroomed like a purple and black bruise. Pinpricks of light flashed in the distance. Wind gusts made her shiver.

Judy trotted over to the barn. Hart hauled in the water hose while she started tossing tools into the wheelbarrow.

"Might be a bad blow, or it might miss us. Hard to tell," Hart hollered over the wind. "But we should pick up any loose things in the yard. Anything can turn into a dangerous weapon if the wind hurls it."

"What about the chickens?"

Hart watched them strutting around, unconcerned but flapping their wings when a gust of wind hit them. "If we have time we can try to put them in the barn. The cattle will be okay. I bedded the calves down in the basement pens."

Judy helped put away the few things left about. Hart tended to work neatly, so there wasn't much to pick up. She took in the few earthenware pots of impatiens that she had set around the barn. A crack of thunder made her jump and throw her arms over her head. Hart came running and grabbed her by the shoulders.

For ten heartbeats the entire farm went still. The wind died, the birds were silent, and there was not a rustle. The sky took on an eerie, pale egg-yolk color.

"Are you okay? Come on, run!" Hart's hand slid down to pull at her arm.

"There's no rain, Hart. How's come there's thunder. . ."

Judy stopped her jog, ignoring Hart's tug on her elbow.

Hart turned in the direction of her stare. "Come on."

Four strides later Judy felt her shoe catch. She went down in a heap, pulling Hart along.

"Judy!"

"I'm okay." Twisting to her knees, Judy reached

back to see what held her shoelace. As if in slow motion she reached for a ring imbedded in the sod. "Hart—"

"What are you doing?" With one last look at the converging maelstrom, Hart pushed her hands away and yanked on the shoelace. A whole square of sod came up with the ring. Hart changed his grip from the entangled lace to the metal ring. Judy didn't hesitate to rip off her shoe and throw herself through the trap door at Hart's urging. They plunged down a mercifully short flight of cement steps into darkness. The door thudded over them.

Judy tumbled to the hard floor and lay gasping for breath in the staleness, the shock of banging her head and seeing stars wearing off. Hart groaned.

"Lady, I've only got a couple of spare ribs to give you." He coughed. "Ahh. I think I'll start charging you. Hey! Judy! Answer me. Are you okay?"

"Mmm, I just—I think I hit my head. I'm a little dizzy. Did I hurt you again?"

"Not bad."

Judy reached in the dark to feel his chest and shoulder. She could smell sweat and old hay as her other senses magnified without the ability to see. "I think we found the bomb shelter."

"I would agree. You sure you're all right?" Hart asked.

"Yes, I think so."

The door above them began to rattle, sending showers of dirt onto the steps. Judy could feel Hart reach around her shoulders. Like stereo bass the ground shook, making the walls of the shelter vibrate. Hart pulled her head down to his chest. A horrific explosion shuddered through the shelter. She felt as though a huge muffler cut them off from the rest of the world.

"Hart?" Judy clung to him. He coughed. "Hart?"

"I'm okay. I think. Unless I'm dead."

A relieved breath whooshed out of her. "I guess that would mean I'm dead, too. And this doesn't seem like heaven."

She felt Hart's arms tighten around her, his hand rubbing along her back. Then both of his warm rough palms moved along her cheeks over her ears, his fingers reaching into her scalp.

"Oww." Judy took a quick breath.

Hart gently explored the bump. "You've got a good-sized goose egg. I don't feel blood." He untangled himself. "This place is so dark, I don't know which way is up."

"It feels clammy in here." She got to her knees and reached toward what she hoped would be a wall. "I know what you mean about not knowing which way is up. Where're the steps? We have to get out of here. Do you think the tornado passed over yet?"

She could hear Hart's work boots shuffle on the cement floor. "I think so," he said from somewhere past her left ear.

Judy put her arms out like a sleepwalker and tried to follow the sound. Her stockinged toe banged hard. "Ow!"

"Now what?"

"I hit something."

"Something?"

Judy leaned over and touched the object. "Feels like a box. Have you ever been in such a dark place? There's no light at all."

"Where—oh, sorry." Hart's outstretched arm whacked her in the shoulder.

"Here." Judy grabbed for his arm and pulled his hand down to touch the box.

"Ouch!"

"Now it's your turn to hit something?"

"I think I picked up a sliver."

"Sorry."

"It's not your fault, but I don't understand. . ." She could hear him moving, tapping on wood. "There's more than one box. And smell that? The wood's fresh."

"But who?—how? Oh." Realization dawned. "I had a little incident last night with trespassing, and Sheriff Danner sent someone out to investigate." Judy rubbed her arms.

"Incident?"

"I planned to tell you about it." Judy reached for a box and gingerly lowered herself to sit. She could feel Hart's warmth as he moved close to her. His hand rested on her shoulder. "I woke up about three or so and heard people in the yard. By the time I got a look they were driving away."

"We're isolated out here. I never felt worried about my own safety, although I suppose I should have been. I never considered the threat of crooks, though I've got nothing of much value. But now you've got me concerned for your safety."

"Thanks. I'll be all right. The deputy thought they were leaving trash or just stopped to make a call."

"You think otherwise?"

"I got the feeling they were looking for something."

"Something like a bomb shelter?"

"But who would know about this unless they knew the family?"

Hart moved away from her again. "These boxes

might give us a clue."

"I suppose. You know, I never noticed that metal ring in the yard, even with the lawn mowing. I don't think it stuck out that far, but maybe with all the rain lately, when the truck drove around the yard last night, the ring was exposed. Especially if this is what they were doing—leaving these crates."

"Could be. . .and I just found the steps."

"Where are you? Keep talking."

"Here. I'm on the steps, reaching the door."

Judy edged forward and ran into a cement step. "Okay. I'm right behind you. I think." She felt Hart's arm on her shoulder, guiding her next to him in the small space.

"There's the door. I've tried to open it, but I think it's stuck. I'll try turning the handle again."

Judy heard a dull jingle as Hart evidently tried to move the handle. She reached up to feel the door for herself. Not even a shimmer of light showed around the edges. "How about I help push?"

"Okay. Are you ready? One, two, three. . .push. Ahhh." Hart panted.

"Hart, I'm so sorry. Are your ribs sore? Can you just sit? I'll shove."

Judy felt him sink down to a step by her ankles. She turned the handle of the hatch and heaved with all of her might. "I—can't—get it to—budge." She dropped down beside him. "Something heavy must have fallen on top of the door."

"The storm has to be over. I don't hear a thing out there. Tornadoes are usually short and wicked."

"I wouldn't know. I've never been in one." Judy stood. "These steps are cold."

"We weren't caught in the tornado, thanks to your quick thinking."

In the dank darkness, she felt claustrophobic, and it hit her that they were trapped. "What if we can't get out?"

"Don't worry. Someone will come to look for us. If they haven't started already." Judy held her breath and clung to Hart's reassurance. "We'll figure this out. Just relax."

Judy carefully maneuvered her way around what felt like a half dozen crates. She handled a rough, heavy canvas bag. "I wonder what's in these crates."

Hart shuffled along behind her. "I guess supplies of some kind. I know underground storage areas were meant to preserve goods."

"Should we try to open one?"

"If you want to. But they're probably closed pretty tight. Oh, sorry." Hart bumped into her.

"That's all right. I feel three—no, four, of these crates piled up back here. I'm going to feel for the—ouch!"

"What's the matter?"

Judy put her finger in her mouth. "Matching slivers. You're right. I feel nails all around. You didn't bring your hammer with you, did you?"

Hart chuckled. "No. How about we sit for a while? Maybe we'll hear someone up there later. We can try calling for help."

Judy felt his hand, still warm despite the natural

chill of the underground chamber, tug on her elbow as he settled himself on a couple of crates. "Here. We can rest. . .keep warm together."

She leaned against him comfortably, warm on one side, chilly on the other. She'd never felt so close to a man she'd known such a short time—certainly not Graham. And as much as she wanted someone to rescue them out of this hole in the earth, she wanted their time together to last.

"Your foot has to be cold," Hart said. "Let me rub it for you."

"That's sweet of you," she said without forethought.

"So I suppose we can't call this a date, can we?" Hart laughed.

Judy tensed for a moment then let out her breath. "I'd at least like candles."

"I'll remember that next time, I promise."

Hart's hand warmed her cold foot. She debated whether or not to remove the wet sock then decided not to. A date? Did Hart mean he'd like to date her? Judy twitched her shoulders again.

Hart stopped his foot rubbing, and she felt his chest expand before he spoke. "So, tell me about teaching school."

Good. A safe topic. "I saw Aunt Louise tutoring kids and giving piano lessons after school. I wanted to do the same, only in a classroom. She helped me through college as much as she could."

"Do you really like teaching?"

"Yes. Well, the job's tough. Kids, parents, everyone always wanting something. In a way, it's nice to be needed. Exhausting, too. But you know, when you see that spark, that first time something makes sense and the kid figures out how things work or why knowledge matters, then giving that piece of yourself becomes worthwhile."

"Sounds like a good job for someone like you," Hart said, and she took the words as a compliment.

Judy curled her legs up and tucked her toes under her knee. "I guess." She listened to his heart beating. The pace quickened as he asked his next question.

"Why were you dating a guy like Graham Montgomery?"

She went still and examined her feelings. What could she say? She'd allowed herself to be hurt by Graham's selfishness. "I was flattered, I guess. At first. He was charming. And he acted interested in me." Judy sat up and started to pull away from Hart.

Hart kept his grasp on her hand. "Hey. Calm down. Come back here. I'm cold." Judy allowed him to tuck her back against his strong shoulder. "You're afraid of him."

She felt his hand in the middle of her back, the heat all the way through to her skin. "No. Maybe a little."

He lifted his chin away from her temple. "What was that?"

"What?"

"That sound."

They both sat in comfortable silence for a while. "I only hear us," Judy finally said.

"Hmm. I guess you're right, but I thought I heard something out there."

The two of them settled back. They alternately talked and tried to listen for a rescue for what felt like the rest of the day.

Hart stroked her hair. "How's your head?"

"Sore," she confessed. "In fact, I'm getting a headache."

Hart's hand slid through her hair, over her ear. "There's no telling how long we'll be down here before someone figures out how to find us and get us out."

"Hart? Would you mind if I asked you to pray for our safety—and those outside?"

"Oh yeah, that would be a good idea, wouldn't it? Glad you thought of it. Why don't you close your eyes while I pray?"

Snuggling deeper against his shoulder, she said, "Mmm, okay."

Judy listened to Hart as she drifted to sleep, the words tumbled together in soothing susurrus.

Judy woke, stiff, but with her head no longer throbbing. She sat up and rubbed her arms.

Hart coughed and cleared his throat. "How are you?"

"You're awake, too. Did you sleep much? I'm feeling better. How are you?"

"I'm fine. Yeah, I slept for a while, I guess."

Panic rose up in her. "We've been down here a long time, Hart. Do you have any idea what time it is?"

"I don't wear a watch when I'm doing chores. You wouldn't believe how often one ends up in a cow's stomach. I wouldn't be able to read it in the dark, anyway." He laughed.

Judy giggled. If Hart was making light of their dilemma, he was probably certain somebody would come to their rescue and she should relax. "A watch in a cow? I wouldn't have guessed. I wonder if we slept, like, all night or something. Maybe by now somebody's figured out we're missing."

"I hope so. Here, let me check your head." Hart ran his hand over her hair.

"Oww." Judy felt Hart's breath on her ear, his fingers gentle on her scalp. They both laughed when his stomach grumbled and hers echoed.

"It must be at least breakfast time," Judy said. Something in her dreams nagged her. "Hart, how well do you know Ardyth?"

"Our Ardyth?"

"Yes. How many other women do you know with that name?"

"I thought your headache was better. Or are you always grumpy when you wake up?"

Judy snorted a self-conscious laugh. "Sorry. I just had a weird dream. I think. I can't remember. But, seriously, have you heard anything about her?"

"What do you want to know?"

"Um, I know what people think of her. She acts a little strange sometimes."

"An understatement. Eccentric."

"Yes, she's definitely eccentric."

"She said she was a secretary for a big financial firm down in St. Louis."

Judy got up to pace a few steps. "And I'm pretty sure she was, and maybe still is, in love with Bryce. I know he never married because of her."

Hart responded with a laugh. "Really?"

Judy hesitated. Maybe her suspicions were bizarre, but she felt compelled to press on. "Mmm, Hart?"

"Yes?"

"Do you think she's the vengeful type? Say, if she thought someone had wronged her, would she do something about it?"

"Ardyth? Do something dangerous?"

Again, doubts assailed, but there was the dream. . . "Maybe."

"What are you talking about, Judy?

"Oh, forget it." Of course little old Ardyth wasn't capable of anything sinister. "I can't believe I even brought up the subject."

With little room for two adults to try the door then pace, they soon returned to sit next to each other. Judy pulled herself to sit cross-legged on a crate, hunched over.

Hart broke the silence first. "I didn't know what to think of you when I first saw you in the orchard. I knew that you were here for the funeral. When I got close, all I could think about was how beautiful you were."

Judy felt shivery. "I'm glad you can't see me now. I must be filthy." She shifted to rest against him again. Hart's arms closed about her. "And there *you* were, Hart, coming at me like some territorial cat."

"Then you fell on me. Knocked some sense into me."

Judy laughed. "Yeah, I'm sorry."

"I think I'd like this adventure in the shelter to be a date after all."

Judy lifted her head. "Oh, you do, huh?"

She felt his body curling and the heat of his face as he lowered his head to hers.

Judy tensed as a rhythmic banging, clanking sound started over their heads. She sat up. "Shh! Wait. Do you hear that?"

"Hey! Anyone there?" A muffled voice echoed.

Judy sat up. "A vent pipe. I never thought of that before." She turned and put a hand out to feel the cast metal jointed tube. "Yes! We're down here! Hart and Judy!"

"Okay," the voice came back. "Just hang on. We're. . ." The roar of an engine cut off the rest.

Judy grasped Hart's arms and laughed. "Oh, I'm so glad. I couldn't imagine anyone who's claustrophobic being stuck in here!"

"Yeah." Hart got up, and she could hear him take a hesitant shuffling step as he got his balance.

Judy found her own feet and grabbed his hand. "Come on, we're getting out!"

"I'm happy, all right? I'm just worried about the. . . cattle and our buildings, and whether anyone else was caught out in the storm."

"People caught in the tornado? The cattle. . .the house." Judy sobered instantly. "I almost forgot there was life outside these walls."

A grinding noise filtered down to them. Soon she could see the outline of the trapdoor. Thumping confirmed it. She and Hart started up the steps.

"Hallo!"

"We're here!" Judy called out.

Hart tugged on her elbow. "Judy, wait. Before we go out, I wanted—"

The door creaked upward, and she blinked at the piercing light. "Art! Boy, am I glad to see you!" Judy heaved a huge mock sigh for their rescuer's benefit. "How long have we been down there?" She helped Hart up the rest of the way then stopped at the sight of the crowd waiting for them. "Oh, my goodness."

"It's going on eleven in the morning. When no one could find you yesterday evening," Art said, "I got to thinking, 'I wonder if they holed up in that old bomb shelter,' see, 'cause we were talkin' about it—"

"There's my Judy. Babe!"

Judy tensed and closed her eyes at the all-too-familiar voice. "Graham!"

"I'm here. Everything's gonna be just fine now."

13

"Hello, Graham. What are you doing here?" Judy looked toward Hart and saw his broad shoulders stiffen before she turned to greet Graham.

They had broken off their relationship, but apparently Graham had forgotten or chose to ignore that fact.

"When I heard there was a tornado in Robertsville, I drove right over," Graham said.

"I'm fine. You don't need to worry about me." Judy gazed around at the crowd standing in the sun, the day bright and fresh, as if nothing had happened. Two tractors had dragged huge sheets of corrugated metal across her yard. Ruth and Art, along with Bryce and a few others she recognized, stood nearby, curious and eager to do anything to help.

Graham grabbed her and swung her in a great bear hug.

"Graham! Graham, don't—"

Ruth Harris moved in and touched Judy's arm then led her toward an ambulance. "Oh, Judy, are you all right? My, that's quite a bump."

"Ruth, I don't need—"

"Just let them take a look, Judy." Bryce took her other arm.

Judy winced while the medic checked her over. He checked her vitals then sprayed something on her scalp, but her thoughts were on Hart. What must he think of her? Cozying up to him in the shelter and then him coming out to see Graham embrace her?

"Just take it easy for a couple of days," the medic said. "And if you have any nausea, come to the clinic immediately. Understand?"

Judy nodded, and the medic moved on to Hart. "Sir? You're injured?"

"His ribs," Judy said. "He—I—broke them a few weeks ago. He might have hurt them again. Where did the tornado go? Was anyone hurt?"

Bryce stepped forward and took her elbow. "Come on, Judy, let's get you inside—get you something to drink and some rest."

"No, thank you." Judy walked backward the first few steps, watching the medic check Hart's breathing and heart. "I won't leave until I know Hart's all right."

Hart held her gaze then waved her away. "I'm fine—perfect. Just go." She looked from Hart to Graham, whose expression was a mixture of caution and jealousy. Graham's rigid posture, his folded arms and set mouth, sent a chill through her. He stood apart from the others, who gave him wide berth when they had to walk by. His stiff nod alerted her to his desire to talk to her.

Bryce continued to guide her toward the house, which was intact despite the mighty winds. She couldn't help a sigh of relief. "So—"

"I imagine you'd like a bathroom break first, young lady." Bryce's eyelids flickered. He held out her missing shoe. "Carranza brought this to me. Looks like yours. Why don't you go freshen up while I get you something to drink and eat?"

Judy snatched her shoe and walked inside after a backward glance at Hart. He looked away from her, and her heart sank.

Ardyth directed traffic in the kitchen, supervising neighbor women who stacked the already groaning kitchen table high with donations of casseroles and breads and cakes.

Judy blinked. "Oh, wow. Ardyth, where did all this come from? I hope nobody thought we were hurt badly. . .or anything."

"Of course not, dear. We knew our prayers would be answered."

Ardyth frowned at Bryce. "Well? What do you want?"

Bryce gave Judy a little push in the direction of the bathroom. "Now, Ardyth," Bryce said, "I'm just here to help."

When Judy returned, Ardyth had apparently left the kitchen. Bryce ushered her into the front parlor, where he'd set a plate of sandwiches and cookies and a salad on the coffee table. "Here, why don't you just lie down for a bit, catch your breath from that crowd."

"Thank you. But what happened with the tornado? Is everyone all right?"

"Funny thing," Bryce said, as he seated himself opposite in a wing chair. "Storm skipped along the fencerow for a while, blew through the yard at my, er, Hart's place, took out the sliding doors from the barn and deposited them in your yard. Right over the bomb shelter. Didn't hit any other buildings, spun up over town and blew out on the highway on the other side."

Bryce helped himself to a cookie. "No one was reported injured. Seems your place and mine took the worst damage." He frowned. "Yup. And funny thing, that young man out there—and I'm not talking about Hart—claims to be your fiancé."

"What? Oh no. We broke up. I don't know why he—"

"There you are, Judy." Graham peered through the front door from the porch. "May I come in? I'll be quiet, I promise."

Judy caught a blur of gray moving down the front hall stairs that faced the entrance. *Carranza.* She held her breath as the attack cat sat directly in front of the door and engaged Graham in a staring contest.

Graham lost. "Can someone please get this cat out of the way?"

Bryce huffed a breath of annoyance and got to his feet. At the door, he paused in the act of picking up Carranza. "Judy's exhausted and needs to rest, young man. What can I do for you? Anything? No? Then perhaps it's best if you leave, son."

Carranza added his agreement in the form of a deep-throated growl.

"Come on, Judy. I just need to talk about. . .about the wedding."

"What wedding?" The throb in her head pounded harder. "Graham, we broke up. I don't have anything to say to you anymore."

"But—but. . .I love you, Judy."

She tried to sit up, but the room swam in front of

her eyes. "Good-bye, Graham."

Carranza growled again in Bryce's arms. "I'll thank you to leave, sir." Bryce closed the oak door with a slam.

Bryce returned to the parlor. He stroked Carranza who made no move to get away. "That young man has a bug about something."

"I don't think it's me, Bryce." Judy shifted on the sofa and closed her eyes. "He admitted he'd visited Louise. He said he wanted to convince her that he was good enough to date me. Louise didn't take an active dislike to him, as far as I knew. I don't understand why he keeps coming here." Judy opened her eyes to gauge Bryce's reaction.

Carranza leapt from Bryce's arms to circle the floor in front of the sofa. He plopped down as if to guard her, tail whapping the floor.

"Judy, you appear to be in good hands at this point. Why don't I shoo the rest of the curious away for now? I'll have Ardyth check up on you later."

Judy yawned. "Okay. Thanks for everything today, Bryce."

"I'll see myself out."

That was the last she knew until the next morning. A ringing phone slowly roused Judy from her stupor. She drew herself up on her elbows and blinked at the sunshine streaming through the window. Dust motes circled with her movement. She slowly twisted to set her feet on the floor and hunched, holding her head. The phone began to ring again.

"All right! I'm coming." Judy moved as quickly as

her aching joints allowed and lifted the receiver. "Good morning."

"Oh, there you are, dear. Did I wake you?"

"Good morning, Ardyth." Judy squinted at the clock on the wall. "Wow. I really slept. I guess I should be up anyway. Thanks again for all you did yesterday. Arranging. . ." Judy turned to survey the loaves of bread and cakes adorning her countertop, and she suspected, filling the refrigerator. "Everything. I appreciate it. Bryce said no one was hurt?"

Ardyth's sniff passed over the line, straight and clear. "That's right. Now, I'll be over in a few minutes to help you get dressed and cleaned up."

"Oh! Th–thank you, Ardyth, but I'm perfectly all right. Hart was in worse shape than me."

"I believe someone's with him today. You sure you don't need me?"

Judy could hear the plaintive tone. Ardyth sounded lonely. "Well, perhaps you could come in an hour or so—help me sort through some of this food. I can't possibly eat it all. Did anyone give any to Hart? We can take some over there."

"As long as that Bryce is gone. Okay, then, I'll see you in about an hour."

As soon as Ardyth hung up, the phone rang again.

Oh, bother. "Hello, Judy speaking."

"Judy, please, it's me, Graham. You've just got to listen to me. You can't tell—"

"Graham, I don't have to listen to you. Now, will you leave me alone? I don't want to talk to you anymore."

"But—"

Judy set the phone in the cradle and then unplugged the cord. Her cell phone had caller ID, so she could see if he tried to call that number. She swiveled her neck and sighed. A shower and change of clothes were first on the agenda. When she turned, Carranza sat directly in her path.

"What have you got there? Don't tell me it's some kind of beetle." Grimacing, Judy leaned down to get a look at what Carranza guarded. Black and shiny, the object looked like some kind of bean. "Where did you get that? You want me to take it away?" When she reached for it, Carranza put a paw over the object.

"You want to play?" Judy stroked his head. "That's not like you. I really don't have time right now."

Carranza blinked then began to slide the bean across the kitchen floor to the back room.

Judy shook her head at the cat's crazy antics and went to get cleaned up.

Ardyth really had been a big help, Judy admitted late that afternoon after her friend had gone home. The big steel barn doors had been picked up and hauled back to Hart's yard, with Bryce's help. She and Ardyth packed up several meals for Hart to freeze and fed the helpers who loaded the heavy doors. Against Judy's protest, Ardyth had dusted and vacuumed the downstairs and dawdled, admiring everything about the new bathroom. Judy grinned at the thought of her sighs when viewing the huge spa tub.

Ardyth had been visiting her brother in Milwaukee when Louise died, which put to rest the last of the secondary suspects on Judy's list. That left Graham or the KOWPIE people. But how to proceed when she couldn't stand to be near Graham?

Judy sat on the front porch, cooling off and watching the sun begin a long fiery descent. She hadn't had a chance to look in the bomb shelter again. Resolved to check it out, she went inside the house for a flashlight. She checked the batteries and hesitated only momentarily before heading out the door.

Graham's little blue car idled noisily in the drive. He shut off the engine then got out slowly, standing by the door. Neither of them said anything at first.

Graham pointed at the flashlight Judy gripped with white knuckles. "Looks like you're going exploring. Let me guess, getting back on the horse again after a fall? Going to check out that creepy shelter?"

He took a step toward her. Judy willed herself not to retreat. "I wouldn't do that if I were you, Judy." Graham took another step. "Why bring up bad memories? Or were they bad? What did you and that guy do down there, anyway, to keep yourselves entertained?"

Out of the corner of her eye, she noticed a pickup truck on the road headed their way. She counted to four in her head, about the time it would take to get within signaling distance of her own driveway if the driver planned to stop. Yes! Hart.

"Graham, I'm asking you politely for the last time to leave me alone. I'll take out a restraining order if I have to. There is no reason for you to keep bothering me." Hart's truck came to a halt behind Graham. They both watched Hart slam the door and stand there, arms folded.

"I'm just trying to help you, Judy. Keep you from nightmares. I care about you and your place, that's all." Without another word, he settled himself back in his car and gunned out of the farmyard.

Hart turned his head back in Judy's direction when Graham's car was out of sight. "Hi. Some sense told me I should come and check on you."

"Is that right?" Judy relaxed the grip she had on the torch and studied the imprint of grooves in her palm.

"So, did you?"

Judy took in the picture Hart made, leaning against his dusty truck, legs crossed casually and arms still folded, before answering. "Did I what?"

"Need my help."

Judy twitched her mouth to the side to keep from laughing. "I would say you came in answer to a prayer, yes."

Hart pushed himself away from the truck and took a few steps toward her. "Judy. Are you all right? Do you want me to call the sheriff?"

"I'll be okay. Thanks." He advanced within touching distance when he stopped to stare at something behind her shoulder. She turned to see what startled him and burst out laughing at the sight of Carranza leading a line of half-grown kittens from the barn. "What is that crazy beast up to now?"

"He seems determined about something. I've never seen a male cat do that before. Did you see the mother cat?"

"No. We'd better go look. Where is he taking them? Better not be the house," Judy threatened. Carranza led his tribe around the basement yard, under the mesh fence, and up the wide drive into the top of the barn.

Hart led her into the lower level, handling the latch like a pro. He flipped the switch. A calf bawled and heaved itself to its feet. Hart fondled the crisp white forehead while they both called "Kitty" to no avail. Judy shone the torch behind some feed sacks and a couple of bales of straw bedding.

"I don't see anything," Judy said and shut off the flash. "We'll chalk up this little episode to Pied Piper cat, up there."

Hart flicked off the light and latched the door behind them. "So, what were you planning to do, anyway, before I got here? Not brain the guy with the light?"

"I was going to check out the bomb shelter."

"With him?"

Judy studied Hart. She couldn't tell by his tone if he felt slightly jealous or if he joked.

"Graham showed up as I was walking out here. It's too dark to look in there now." The excuse sounded so lame she could hardly believe she uttered it. Of course, the shelter was dark all of the time, being underground and all. Thankfully, Hart didn't say a word but walked toward his truck. Judy got the feeling that Graham didn't want her going in the shelter. If Graham was still hanging around, she didn't want him to see her messing around any more. She'd put her errand off until tomorrow. She wondered if Hart would come with her.

Hart walked toward his truck. "Well, I'd better be going."

"Would you like to stay for a while?" Judy blurted. "I didn't even ask how you're doing. Do your ribs hurt much?"

Hart paused. "I'm fine. A little sore. Your head?"

She couldn't help but smile. "Okay. Only hurts when I touch it."

Hart nodded. "I've got a deacon's meeting tonight. At church. I planned to stop here for a couple of minutes, but I don't want to be late." He waved, hopped into his truck, then headed out of the driveway toward town.

There was so much she'd meant to say, but the words didn't come. Too late.

Judy stared at the encroaching cloudbank, dark behind the billowy bright front.

A light rain shower began as the sun disappeared and kept up an intermittent patter all evening. Judy snuggled in her own bed, grateful for her fluffy mattress. Not that leaning against Hart's warmth had been all that bad. She'd barely felt the couch last night, she'd been so tired.

Judy punched her pillow and rolled onto her side. A rehash of Graham's visit played. Why did he continue to pester her?

Plop. Plop. Plink.

What could he possibly want from her? Surely there were plenty of other fish in Lewiston. Like that Rachel from school.

Plink. Plop. Plink.

And what was that sound? Had she left the faucet running downstairs? Judy sat up in bed. The annoying sound was close. She reached for the bedside lamp and turned the switch.

Judy got up and padded toward the door and hall. No, she couldn't hear—wait! She turned back toward the window. No. It must be coming from the closet. The floor was damp in front of the closet door. She opened the door cautiously to see the drip plop from the upper corner of the ceiling onto a gathering pool on the wood floor.

"I guess I do need a new roof. What next?" Judy went downstairs to get a bucket from the mudroom. She trudged up the stairs, Carranza on her heels, and set the bucket under the leak.

Drops clanging into the galvanized bucket made such a racket that she knew she'd never sleep. After soaking up as much moisture as she could from the floor, she grabbed her pillow and blanket and went down to the lumpy sofa she'd slept on the night before.

Her heavy eyelids began to droop when a new sound assailed her senses. Sitting bolt upright, Judy held her breath in the dark. Now what?

A sharp *crack* and *pop* yanked her upright off the couch. Clutching the afghan to her chest, Judy turned in the pitch-dark, fumbling on her knees for the switch to the floor lamp. A growl and a hiss sent her reeling back to the sofa. "Carranza! Stop it!"

The raggedy cat leaped on something in the middle room between the kitchen and living room. Judy watched his antics through the French doors. Carranza growled again and began to pat at something on the floor.

"Did you catch a mouse? Clever boy. Take it out now." She was in no mood for his strange gifts tonight. Or was it morning? Judy yawned. "Take it out, Carranza. And you can stay out, too, for that matter. Please, let me sleep!"

Carranza began to slide something across the floor. Just like the other day. Judy walked into the other room. "Stop. Let me see. What have you got? A bean . . .like before. Where did you get this?" She ignored his hiss and plucked the shiny black bean from the floor. She rubbed it thoughtfully, revealing a faint pattern on the sides. She stared into space. Where had she seen something like this before?

14

Judy buttoned her blouse. The thought of a visit to Lewiston held no pleasure for her. That more than anything else convinced her that even if Louise's death was never atoned for, Judy's home was the Jamison farmstead. The spruced-up house, spectacular tub, job offer, and a certain handsome neighbor were gravy to balance the equation. But she had no intention of giving up her own personal inquest into the last few months of Louise's life. The diaries proved entertaining but not terribly newsworthy. Louise seemed to find more fault with her friends as time went on. There had been a huge gap of three empty months last spring.

Judy's drive was uneventful, and, in the end, moving to the farm was easy enough. Her apartment lease in Lewiston went month to month. She didn't have much to pack up. Tanya, her neighbor, claimed several pieces of furniture and promised to find good homes for the other things Judy wouldn't take. The landlord had been very accommodating. Next stop: her job.

She arranged to talk to the principal at school. Once settled in his office, Mr. York let her know he was unhappy with her desire to resign.

"I'd prefer to think of this as a leave of absence. You've been the cream of the new crop, Miss Winters. We've come to rely on your certain talents, besides your gifted control of your classroom. You will not be easily replaced."

Judy had her doubts but was grateful for the man's comments. "Thank you, Mr. York. I'll miss Lewiston and my friends, but I plan to keep in touch."

"You do that, Miss Winters."

Judy cleaned out her desk, stopped to say farewell to various staff members she'd gotten to know, and put out one last general e-mail to her colleagues explaining that she had decided to move to her family home across the state and take a new job. After she'd pressed the SEND button, she realized that the message automatically went into Graham's mailbox, too.

The return trip to Robertsville barely registered. Hart had agreed earlier to help her unload her car after chores.

She stopped him when he reached for one of several cartons of books. "Wait, Hart. I'll get those later. I don't want you to strain your ribs."

He stretched to heft one, in spite of her warning. With a sharp intake of breath, he let the box settle back on the car seat. "Okay. I give up. Got anything lighter?"

Cradling an armful of houseplants, Judy restrained a grin and handed him her laundry basket.

"Where to?" Hart headed for the house.

"I guess the dining room for now. You can set it on the floor by the window."

She had just entered the kitchen with a box of paper goods from the apartment when Hart called to her from the dining room. "Hey, Judy?"

She set the box on the table and walked through the open French doors. "Yes?"

He fingered the tall, shiny-leafed houseplant.

"Where did you get this?"

"It was here when I came. Isn't it pretty? It used to have red flowers."

Hart huffed out a breath. "It's a castor bean plant. And the seeds are popping. Didn't anyone tell you how dangerous these things are?"

"Dangerous?" She frowned and folded her arms. "What do you mean? What's dangerous?"

Hands loose on his hips, Hart shook his head. "The beans come shooting out, for one thing. For another, they're *deadly* poisonous."

"Poisonous?" Judy backed away from the plant. "To humans? To animals? You're kidding. Carranza has been. . . Carranza! Carranza, where are you?" Panic spiked as she called for her cat. Judy looked at Hart. "You don't think. . . Carranza!"

Hart followed her around the house, calling the cat's name. When she rushed back to the kitchen on her way outside, she nearly tripped over the animal. "There you are! Are you all right?" She reached out to pick him up, but Carranza backed up, twitching his ears and whiskers.

"He looks fine," Hart said.

"You think so?"

Carranza sat then licked a paw for his audience. After a few deliberate yowls of displeasure, he stalked through the mudroom.

"You've gotta get rid of that plant, Judy. Don't burn it, just uproot it somewhere and let the roots dry up."

Judy eyed the dangerous plant. "But where is a safe place to leave it?"

"Maybe. . .how about we take it to that shed at the back of the barn? Or better yet, why don't you let me take it back to my place? I don't have any animals that would get into it."

"Would you?" She gave the deadly plant a sideways glance and shuddered. "I'd appreciate it."

A half hour later, Judy walked Hart to the door. "I appreciated your help today, Hart."

"Just being neighborly." Hart winked. "I saw your name on the picnic committee at church, by the way."

Judy could see the amber flecks in his eyes, as he waited with his hand on the doorknob. She smiled tentatively at him. "Those church ladies just have a way of putting a body to work without you hardly noticing."

Hart's hand came down on hers, his head tilted to the side. "Should we go together?"

"To the picnic?"

"Yeah, that's what I'm asking."

Dare she say it? Judy tilted her chin. "You're asking me out, Hart?"

"Yeah." Hart's slow smile nearly melted her heart. "Third date. You planned to go to the picnic, didn't you?"

Smiling at him, she was hit again with the sense that now that she had made the move to Robertsville, they'd be permanent neighbors. Judy cleared her throat. "I'm helping with the food. I've got to be there."

Hart pursed his lips. "I can help, too."

"Okay, then." Hart was close enough that she could feel his body heat. He leaned in and brushed his mouth across the bruise at the edge of her hairline. "I'll be back tomorrow to pick you up."

As good as his word, Hart returned the next morning to help carry her things to his truck. "Somewhere it's got to be ordained that all church picnics can only take place on sunny, dry days," he remarked.

"I agree." Judy noticed they had chosen to wear nearly the same color beige denim slacks. Hart's dark brown polo emphasized the tan he'd picked up from his outdoor work. What would people think when they arrived together? The thought didn't have time to root as they pulled up to the church and she was immediately put to work in the kitchen while Hart lent a hand setting up chairs outside.

"What do you do if the weather isn't this fabulous?" Judy asked the assembled group in the church kitchen.

"Find out who didn't say their prayers and give him or her twenty lashes with a wet noodle," Kathy Tyson, the pastor's wife, joked. "Judy, where's that big tub of mustard and mayo? I'm ready to add the potatoes."

Judy wiped her streaming eyes with a paper towel, compliments of the onions. She retrieved the mustard and mayo then picked up the cutting board and used the side of her knife to slide her chopped onions into the big bowl of potato salad.

Kathy used both hands to stir the onions into the mix. "Mm-hmm, I just love this day."

Judy watched while Kathy stirred the salad. "I've never seen such a big bowl."

"Oh, this will be gone by the middle of the second pass, don't worry," Kathy said and looked toward the doorway. "Hart. Just in time. Can you carry this out to the tables, please?"

"Sure thing." Hart grinned at the sight of Judy, whose eyes were still watering. "Onion duty, I see."

"Yup." Judy sniffled and went to rinse the cutting board and wash the knife in the soapy dishwater. "Do you usually get a big turnout for the picnic?"

"Always," Kathy and Mary Tennison said simultaneously.

The sound of rattling knives cutting pickles and radishes, the plop of barbecue being ladled into crock pots, and the huge coffeepots perking made for a joyful symphony.

"Here's the big spoon, Judy. Why don't you follow Hart outside and make sure every dish has a serving spoon? Then you two can enjoy yourselves for a while. When the line starts running low, we'll put some of the perishables away. I'll signal everyone later for KP duty."

The sight of Hart talking to Bryce, Ralph Tennison, and John Walters made her take in a breath. Handsome was more than skin deep, and she had come to admire his willingness to work hard, his sensitivity and desire to make himself useful in any situation.

Judy walked around the serving table, checking to make sure that all the dishes had a spoon or spatula. The delicious aromas made her mouth water.

Pastor Tyson called out that it was prayer time. Judy went to join Hart, who held out his hand and drew her to his side. A verse came to her mind: "In all things God works for the good of those who love him, who have been called according to his purpose."

As they made their way along the buffet line, Judy's conscience assailed her. Was she following God's will in her life? She was troubled by the niggling thought that she was waiting for something to happen to spoil her happiness.

Judy and Hart found places to sit on one side of a long table covered in white paper. Bryce settled beside Ardyth, opposite Judy and Hart. Their other friends slowly filled in empty spaces.

"Hey, did you hear that Adam Borden passed on?" A sandy-haired burly man brought his plate over to their table and sat down across from Bryce. "Ray Billings," he said, nodding to introduce himself.

"Say, that was the son of old gold-hunting Joe, wasn't he?" Ralph Tennison asked. "I remember that time, 'way back when." He dug an elbow into Bryce's side with a chuckle. "Yep, time's passed since we were in school, hasn't it, old man?"

Ruth Harris clucked. "You boys! I declare. Your foolish notions and all. Following that old man's tales and looking for adventure."

"That was quite a summer, wasn't it, Bryce? With all that excitement going on. Then there was old Harold, bringing home his bride," Ralph said.

Judy and Hart shared a glance.

"Let's see now. Harold brought back a wife, and you, there, Bryce, now—what did you come back with?" Ray teased.

Bryce lifted his Styrofoam coffee cup to his lips.

"Harold got the best deal, don't you think?"

"Oh, I don't know." Ardyth had been quiet until then. Judy cocked her head, watching the gray-haired woman through narrowed eyes. "Rumor had it that you brought back your weight in gold dust." Ardyth's eyebrows were lost under her curled bangs, her lips thin.

Judy shifted uncomfortably against the warm back of the metal folding chair. Hart's fingers came to rest on her shoulder in a silent hint to just sit and listen.

Ralph tapped a finger alongside his nose. "Say, I almost forgot about that."

His wife nudged him. "Help me pick up plates, won't you?" Ralph mock-frowned and lifted his shoulders. "Duty calls."

"You did have some, then?" Ray asked. "I thought the gold was just a story."

"Oh, he did, all right." Ardyth sniffed. "Wouldn't show anyone. Then he lost it." Her nose went in the air. Judy started to learn forward. Hart's hand gripped her shoulder and she sat back.

"I still have your letters, you know, and the postcards you sent, bragging," Ardyth said. "Though why I kept them, moved them around through all the years, I can't imagine."

Ruth Harris excused herself, a worried set of her mouth, but Ray Billings continued to stab at his carrot cake, eagerly attentive.

"You really lost your gold?" Ray said to Bryce through a mouthful. "Where's it now?"

Judy stared at him, eyes wide. Hart's shoulders

convulsed next to her and she poked him, forcing her own mouth to stay straight. Ardyth looked away.

"Lost, Ray. That means I don't know what happened."

"Doncha got insurance or something?"

"No, Ray."

Undaunted, Ray continued. "So, what's it like? Camping in the wilderness, hunting for gold, I mean. How much did you get?"

"You use a shallow pan, Ray, that's why it's called *panning* for gold. Harold and I panned in a stream off the Yukon. We waded in cold water, our feet numb and our pants rolled up, and we swished water around in a shallow pan until flakes of gold settled to the bottom. Then we sloshed out more water and picked out flakes. It takes a long time to even get enough flakes to sneeze at."

"You did that all summer? Whaddya eat? Where'd ya sleep?"

"We had a camp, and we went into town once in a while. Fishing was good. Berries wild and big as your thumb all over the place."

"Man, that's something you'd remember all your life." Ray continued to eat and let Ruth refill his coffee cup. Bryce shook his head at her when she came around the table. Judy turned to see if Kathy had signaled for help to begin clearing away the buffet yet. Judy didn't see anyone who might need her help.

"Then Uncle Harold met Aunt Una, right?" she asked.

Bryce nodded.

"Too bad she didn't have a sister for you," Ardyth said.

Bryce looked over at the kids playing games in the yard. The three-legged race was going on. "She did."

Ardyth snorted.

"I told them I had a girl back home, so I wasn't interested."

"If you're referring to me, that's a load of malarkey!" Ardyth hissed.

Bryce sighed. Judy met Hart's eyes. He just hugged her gently, shaking his head.

"Jenny, you may have saved my letters, but did you read them?"

"Don't call me that old pet name. Of course I read them. I also knew what you did, what you and Harold did, before you left on your little adventure. How dare you treat me like—like chattel!"

Hart slid back from the table, and Judy started to rise.

"Oh no. Stay, please." Ardyth commanded. "Let's get this out, once and for all. You have a stake in this, too, Judy, because of your aunt and uncle. You and Hart should hear."

Judy grimaced and stared at the table, twirling her fingertip on the surface. She noticed that Ruth hovered with the coffeepot at a table just beyond them. Tom St. George, Pastor, Kathy Tyson, and few others sat there, faces turned in their direction.

"Most girls would be flattered to have more than one suitor," Bryce said, staring straight at Ardyth.

"Suitors? Is that what you called yourselves? Honestly. What gives you the idea that I was even interested in either of you? And for your information, a girl's feelings are not something you can make a bet over."

"I've apologized how many ways, Ardyth. But you don't understand, and I can't make you listen to what you don't want to hear. Anyway, you moved on with your life, didn't you?"

"I sure did. Got my own family to prove it, too, while you—you. . ." Ardyth's hands began to shake. She got up and walked away.

Bryce looked in apology at Hart and Judy and shrugged. "At least we're talking." He eyed Judy. "So she told you about our past?"

Judy nodded. "Yes. Awhile ago."

Bryce sighed. "I told you once that I'd been a foolish young man. Maybe I haven't changed much, but I'll set the story straight. I carved those letters in the tree. I put Harold's name on it, too, to remind us how close we all were. We were at the end of an era, going into adulthood, and who knew what changes would come, if we'd all be separated and never see each other again. I meant no harm. I just wanted to remember the good times."

"How did Ardyth get the idea that you'd made a bet?" Hart asked.

Bryce moved the saltshaker around the table in a circle in front of him. "I, ah, may have written something like that. In a letter to her. As a joke."

"Oh, Bryce." Judy leaned over Hart to touch his arm. "You mailed it?"

"Only after Harold had gotten himself engaged. I wrote something about how he'd lost the race for the gold, but I'd won the girl back home. I never dreamed she'd get so sore. When she saw the carving on our tree, well, you can tell how she felt. Harold took my last letter to her home. The one where I. . .never mind. We thought she'd get mail faster that way."

Ruth had edged back, coffeepot still in hand. "You tried to make her listen, Bryce. We all knew how you felt when you got back. That girl is just stubborn, stubborn, stubborn."

Bryce's mouth turned down. "Well, that's something, I guess. Thanks, Ruthie." He thunked the saltshaker on the table. "So much water under the bridge. A person can't make amends after all these years. Foolish. Impossible." Bryce shook his head, pushed his chair back, and got up.

"You'll find nothing is impossible, friends," Pastor Tyson said, a great smile across his face, "with God, that is."

Kathy finally gave the signal for the ladies to begin clearing the dishes from the buffet. Judy fairly ran to the kitchen to hide the tears that had come when poor Bryce had poured out his heart to all who'd listen.

———

Hart drove back to the farm late in the afternoon, apparently in no hurry. Judy let her head fall back against the seat. A breeze through the open window pulled on damp tendrils at her neck.

"Had a good day?" Hart asked. "I did."

"Very good. Thank you for taking me."

Hart carried in the two big platters Judy had been asked to bring. She was told they'd been used for church functions throughout recent memory.

"Just set them on the stove. Thanks. I'll put them away later." Judy refrigerated the boxed-up leftovers Kathy had insisted she take home. Hart stood by the kitchen table, watching her.

Judy kept her distance, feeling a tremble in her fingers. "Would you like some coffee?"

He shook his head. "I'd better check on things then get home. Red and I plan to join forces for baling straw from our winter wheat. Thanks again for coming with me today."

Judy followed him through to the back door where he hesitated, fingering the hook and eye latch on the screen door. "Um, Judy?"

His eyes crinkled in a smile, which set her pulse to racing. "Yes?"

"Would it be okay, on our third date, that is, for me to—"

Before he could turn all the way around, Judy flung herself in his direction and planted her lips on his.

She could feel Hart's smile. "Hey, there." He settled himself against the door frame while reaching around to gather her with a firmer grip. After another delicious lip-lock, Hart leaned back to look in her eyes. "Well, I was going to say 'ask you out again,' but. . ."

Judy felt herself flushing. She bowed her forehead against his chin.

Hart squeezed gently. "So, will you?"

"Mmm-hmm."

15

Judy settled the black handset of the kitchen phone in its cradle. She tapped it a couple of times with a fingernail while staring out the new window that Clyde had put in the back wall. The window let in a lot of morning light, making the cavernous kitchen seem almost cheery. Gene Reynolds was right about the vintage look, and Judy had elected not to replace the cupboards. Clyde had agreed to find all the mouse holes and fill and patch them.

Another chunk of wood came flying down even as she looked outside. The crew had already removed the old roof all the way to the sheathing and replaced most of the base. Clyde had a group of young men up there today. She could barely hear them from the first floor as they nailed new shingles over the rubber mat.

Judy looked back at the telephone. This was the fourth time in the last two days that Ardyth had not answered her phone. Her answering machine didn't pick up, either. Judy decided to drive in and check on her.

Lois Birdseye, Ardyth's next-door neighbor, answered Judy's knock on Ardyth's door.

"Hello, dear. How are you today?"

"Hello, Lois. I'm fine. Is everything all right with Ardyth? I can't seem to get her on the phone."

"How thoughtful of you to ask, dear. I'm sure Ardyth would be so grateful to know that her friends are concerned. She asked me to look after Cat while she had to go home. I thought I'd give the plants a drink, too." Lois wrinkled her nose. "She didn't tell me to, but"—she waved an arm full of jingly charm bracelets—"you know." Her voice dropped to a whisper. "She can be a little forgetful."

Ardyth, forgetful? Judy didn't think so, but she was sure the plants wouldn't mind a watering. She sniffed. "Is there something burning?"

Lois's eyes went wide and she backed into the house. "I'd better go and check."

"Wait!" She didn't care if Lois was cooking bacon at Ardyth's house. "Where's Ardyth?"

"She's in St. Louis," Lois called from inside. "Visiting her daughter. Some sort of emergency, I think."

Judy lingered in the doorway for a while and peeked in, but all was quiet. It wouldn't be right to enter Ardyth's home uninvited, so she turned away and walked toward the library. She saw Bryce coming out of the hardware store. "Bryce, I'm so glad to run into you."

"Hi there, how are you?"

"Doing well, thanks."

Bryce took her arm. "What makes you glad to run into an old man, now?"

"I just came from Ardyth's house. Lois told me there was an emergency in the family. Do you know anything about that?"

"Mrs. Belters does not confide in me. I should think you'd be aware of that."

"Oh. I just wondered if you'd heard she went out of town. Lois said something about a family emergency."

"No, I'm sorry. I don't know anything about it."

They sauntered along the block, enjoying the pleasant day. "Bryce, about the other day, at the church picnic. . ." They came to a stop in front of a statue of the town founder, planted solidly in the middle the walk, surrounded by a patch of nodding pink-and-white-striped petunias.

"What you did back then isn't anyone else's business," Judy said.

"That's mighty thoughtful of you. I just don't want you to think of your uncle and me as a couple of gigolos."

Judy laughed. "Of course not. The thought never occurred to me."

"I appreciate that. You see, Jenny—ah, Ardyth—and Harold and I, well, we all grew up cozy, like brothers and sister. I can't remember not loving her." He shook his head and toed a petunia with one foot.

"Ornery, stubborn as she was, she was always my girl. I guess just in *my* mind."

"She came back here to Robertsville after all this time." Judy winked. "And she *is* widowed."

Bryce stared at her, mouth turned down, then pushed his lip out. "Little Judy, I believe you're letting me in on a big secret."

Judy laughed. "I don't think you miss much. She'd probably be grateful to know that you, um, are concerned about what happens in her family."

"Perhaps you're right."

"She was a bit annoyed that you didn't call on her when she first moved back last winter."

"Can you blame me?" Bryce waved his hand in a dismissive gesture.

"Yes, I can blame you," Judy said. "Sure, she was mad. She kept it bottled up for forty-some odd years. I would think that says something about how deeply she feels about you. And I don't think I'm betraying any confidence by telling you this."

Bryce stirred the flowers again with his boot. "I'm just an old bachelor with no idea of how to treat a lady."

Smiling, Judy draped her arm around his frail shoulders. "Phooey."

He clasped his hands behind his back and turned to look down the street. His shock of white hair blew across his forehead. "Any idea when she gets back?"

"None. Let's keep watch."

Bryce escorted her back to her car. "You've got a sweet spirit, Miss Judy. Yes, indeed. I'm delighted to know that you'll be living in the family home."

"Thanks, Bryce. I feel good about the decision."

"I just wish there had been one last thing I could have done for Louise."

"Well, maybe there is." Judy leaned against her car, soaking up the sunshine and plotting as fast as she could before broaching the idea. "I've been trying to figure out how I could talk to someone from that organization Aunt Louise wanted to leave the farm to. Those KOWPIE people? No one seems to know a name or address or anything." Judy fiddled with her purse, stalling to summon courage. "I heard they've got a headquarters somewhere up near Rice Lake. They've been staging protests. I wonder if you would drive up that way sometime. With me?"

"A hunting expedition of our own?" Bryce wasn't smiling despite the lightness of his comment.

"I guess. I just want to find out more. Why they wanted our farm for their headquarters."

"Young lady, I think I could manage a day to go out of town with you. When would you like to go?"

"How about this weekend? Can you check your schedule?"

Bryce let his head roll back on his neck and squinted at the sky before facing her. "My schedule book says I'm free."

Judy took a turn studying the cotton-ball clouds. "It does, does it? I should keep my schedule so free and breezy."

Bryce rewarded her with a laugh of his own. Judy got into her car and started the engine. "I think I'll stop by Hart's before I go home. We're still looking for something you lost, once upon a time."

"Thank you, child."

"I also had some water damage from the storm. Clyde's putting on a new roof, but I have a leak in my closet that I don't want to bother him about. I'm sure Hart can help me figure out how to fix the wall."

"That he can. I've noticed young Mr. Wingate can handle those pesky upkeep chores by the way he's taken on my old house out there. Always offers to repair this or that. Even replaced a window in the dining room."

"Yes, that sounds like Hart," Judy said a bit too wistfully—and got a knowing wink from Bryce.

Hart agreed to stop in later that evening to take a look at the damaged wall. Judy kept a picture of him in her mind, of how he looked hard at work finishing the cattle pens. In heavy work gloves and boots, he and Red had been installing the gate when Judy stopped her car. He'd planted a slightly gritty kiss on her cheek. Judy fingered her cheek while she waited for Hart to come by, a goofy little smile making her laugh at herself.

Judy made certain that her room was spotless and the bedclothes straightened. She had a fan whirring to dispel some of the summer heat. How much would air conditioning cost? Clyde could tell her.

Hart rapped on her screen door not long after supper.

"Hi, Hart, come on in," Judy called out from the kitchen. She'd been wiping down the counter, wearing a dish towel around her neck. Hart entered the kitchen and immediately grabbed the towel ends to pull her into a much more satisfying kiss than the one from the afternoon.

"Hello to you, too," he said. "You've got a smudge on your cheek."

"Tell me you don't greet everyone like that."

"Nope. Just you. Are you ready to show me your wet wall?"

"Sure, it's upstairs, like I said."

She led the way to her room, where he glanced around briefly before using her flashlight to examine the empty closet. Earlier she'd stashed her things in the room across the hall.

"I think you'll want a whole new wall here, Judy. Water did seep down. See the stains? And it feels damp. The floor is sound. Good hard maple. Do you want me to do the work for you? I can pick up drywall and mud."

"Mud?" Judy watched as he carefully pressed against the wall and mopboard.

He looked up at her from his crouch. "That's the stuff used to join the pieces to make a seamless wall."

"You can do that? I don't know when Clyde could get to this, and I hate to ask, 'cause he's so busy. Can I help? I'd love to learn more about taking care of things. Bryce says you do a good job at his—your—house."

Hart straightened and handed the light to her. He regarded her with a gentle smile, creases fanning from his eyes. "Of course. When do you want to get started? I'd like to visit my folks for a couple of days. And I've been in touch with the university about starting back, maybe even next semester."

"You sound busy. I shouldn't have asked."

Hart took her hands. "I didn't mean for you to think I'm too busy to help. We have to work the third crop of hay soon, but your project, if you help, shouldn't take more than a couple of days. You can even paint it when it's dry." He squeezed her hands. "Probably just need the step stool this time."

Judy wrinkled her nose with a snorting chuckle. "Got it."

"So, how about we find a tape measure and I go tomorrow to pick up supplies? We can tear out the old wall and go from there."

When the phone rang that evening, Judy picked up to hear an excited and breathless Ardyth.

Ardyth, as was her custom, just started right in talking as if she'd only left Judy a moment ago.

"I feel silly. A romance at our age," Ardyth gushed. "I'm seventy-four! And a widow. What am I going to do with a boyfriend?"

"Ardyth! Slow down. And welcome back. Now, what boyfriend? Don't tell me you met someone in—"

"No, no, of course not. And I have you to thank. Imagine. After all this time. Why, I can hear them all now, down at Clarinda's Salon during my regular style. They'll think we're nuts."

"Who's nuts, Ardyth? And did you solve your family crisis?"

"Crisis? Oh, that. Yes, well, Evvie decided she was going to run away. My daughter just needed a little support. All over now. And when I got home, who should be waiting? With flowers and everything?"

Judy wondered if her head would split with the effort of deciphering Ardyth's prattle, but she was beginning to get a whiff of understanding. "Who, Ardyth?"

"Why, Bryce, of course. And we talked and talked. Like a couple of teenagers. I just can't believe. . ."

And on and on. Judy began to clock-watch at Ardyth's third description of the bouquet.

"But I still don't know what I'm going to tell my friends. Honestly, Judy, what am I going to do with a boyfriend?"

Judy giggled with her, answering the repeated question. "Same thing I'd do with a boyfriend. Hug him and kiss him and hold him tight. I'm glad you're back, Ardyth, and happy that you and Bryce are working things out."

⁓

The next day Judy pushed her bedroom furniture to the side and lined up the biggest garbage bin with Uncle Harold's saw and hammer. When Hart arrived in the early afternoon, they explained to Clyde about the closet. Clyde's unusual gruffness betrayed his disappointment that she'd not asked him first.

"I'm so sorry, Clyde," Judy said while Hart dragged two sawhorses together and set the sheets of drywall nearby. "You're busy, and this was just a little bitty project. I'll make sure to always ask you for help in the future."

Placated somewhat, Clyde climbed back up on her roof and was soon happily slamming away with the nail gun. She and Hart pried out the old soft backboards. Hart had removed the door and turned off the electricity to that section of the house. "You never know what kind of wiring job was done in these old places." A battery-operated lantern served as their light source, casting shadows high up to join the recesses above the door.

"I think we have to yank the mopboard off the back wall, too," Hart said. "It's a little damp along the floor. I think the floor itself will be okay."

"I can do that." Judy took the claw hammer from him. "Why don't you sit? Your ribs must bother you still."

Carranza padded in silently just as Judy settled her safety goggles. He trotted right up to Hart and sat, twitching his whiskers as if silently urging her to get to work.

The space accommodated all of her, but to get the best grip on the mopboard, her rear end stuck out the door. "Humph. Well, excuse my best side." Judy stuck her head and shoulders into the closet, crawling on her hands and knees. Then she hammered in the pry bar as she'd seen Hart do and gave it a good yank. The old painted board came free on the third tug.

"Hey! There's something back here." Judy pulled off the goggles, twisted to draw the lantern close, then reached a hand in to pull out the rectangle of yellowed paper.

Hart maneuvered to a position just outside the closet. Carranza wormed his way right inside and sniffed at the paper.

"It's an envelope." Hart stated the obvious then took it when Judy offered. "The letter's stamped. Did you notice the addressee?"

Judy nodded. "We should give this to Ardyth. I don't believe the letter was ever mailed."

"I wonder if this isn't the letter Bryce sent from Alaska with Harold when he brought Una home. He must have stashed it for safekeeping in this closet then lost it behind the board. Poor Ardyth."

"Poor Bryce," Judy countered. "This was one of

the causes behind so much misunderstanding."

"Maybe we should tell Bryce first. He might have changed his mind."

Carranza went to explore behind Judy.

"Actually, Hart, a little bird told me that the wind might have changed in that direction."

Carranza stepped right over her to plop in Hart's lap. "What are you talking about?"

"Ardyth had to visit her family in St. Louis. She didn't tell me, and when I got worried about her, I went to her house. Anyway, Lois was there and told me where Ardyth had gone. On my way home, I ran into Bryce and we sort of. . .well, had a good talk."

"Playing matchmaker?" Hart took her hand and began to caress her knuckles.

"Mmm, that's nice, Hart. Anyway, when Ardyth got home, actually that night, Bryce was waiting for her. Apparently they had a—" Carranza, tired of being ignored, pushed his furry head up to meet their joined hands. "Carranza! Anyway, a heart-to-heart talk. So now, they've, um. . . Hart. . ."

Hart continued to nibble at her fingertips. "Yes?"

Bryce and Ardyth's reunion could wait. "Never mind."

16

Judy and Hart couldn't agree about who should receive the letter. They did agree to wait to mention it, as Judy planned to have everyone over when her house was finished to celebrate both her new job and the remodeling project. Maybe then she and Hart could show both Bryce and Ardyth what they'd found. Hart agreed to the plan, as long as he supervised the meal.

"I don't mind making dinner, Hart," Judy said as she walked him out to his truck. "I can cook something. I'll look in one of Una's old recipe books. How hard can it be?"

"Just don't get carried away. I'll help, okay?"

Judy gave him a playful nudge. "Okay, but I hope you're not insinuating that I'm not a good cook."

Hart gave her a gentle kiss in response and then offered to pray for them both for wisdom. They stood at arm's length while he gave thanks, offered his gratitude for their relationship, and asked for guidance and traveling mercies.

Judy echoed out loud while privately adding her own prayer of gratitude for this man who had come into her life.

———

Hart's absence for a few days would work to her advantage, after all. She and Bryce could get their little trip up north out of the way, and she wouldn't feel obligated to confess to Hart that she'd asked Bryce instead of him to help her find the KOWPIE people. Not that she wanted to keep secrets from Hart. He wanted as badly as she did to know what really happened to Louise.

That doctor Bradshaw from the hospital hadn't yet had a chance to do the research he promised. Judy had called twice, but since the tornado, life had become rushed and topsy-turvy.

When Judy thought about spending time with Hart, her knees turned to mush. She tended to let her mind wander into fluffy little daydreams when he was near, and she wanted no distractions if she found a Woodsman to talk to. Just a peaceful, nonconfrontational discussion about their headquarters. Hopefully in public. Surely no one would object to that?

Hart left Robertsville the next morning for a long weekend. He'd dropped off a message in her paper box with his emergency contact information.

"I'll be here, at my parents' house until Sunday. Then I have an appointment Monday at the university with the long-distance learning people. . . . I'll miss you. Hold the fort until I get back, okay? And don't go any higher than the stepladder in the closet. Love, Hart."

Judy returned to the house after collecting the note and the morning news. She sighed over the "Love, Hart" part of the note, closed her eyes, and decided to focus on the trip.

"Okay, what to wear for a showdown with militant

environmentalists?" Tourist garb. Shorts might do. She also donned a floppy hat, sneakers, and looped a camera strap around her neck.

Bryce came by to pick her up for the drive north. At a gas-station stop, Bryce happened to overhear an exciting tidbit of news.

"A gentleman in there was talking about a parade today in a little place 'bout ten minutes from here. The group got a permit under false pretenses. He seemed upset. I guess his wife sits on the council who issued the permit, and he didn't like seeing her name associated with this. Anyway, the outfit behind the parade sounds like our gang. I think we can park somewhere out of the way, watch, and maybe find one of the organizers afterward."

"Sounds like a plan, Bryce. Let's go."

The town turned out to be one of those "two-streeters" with more bars and gas stations than houses. Bryce parked on the outskirts of the community, on an unpaved road with no sidewalks, typical of rural "up north" Wisconsin.

"I don't understand why KOWPIE would put on a parade here. There's nothing around," Judy said while the two of them hiked toward one of the main intersections.

"Just tourists. You did notice how many cars were parked at the lake, didn't you? The city park's full, too."

They rounded the corner and Judy's eyes widened when she saw how many people lined the street. "Where did they all come from?"

"That's the way it works in the summertime. I

suspect those fellows think they can get their agenda across by disrupting tourism. I don't like this. Feels funny," Bryce said.

A barefoot young woman in cutoffs toting an infant stepped out of a rundown building just to Judy's left. A motorcycle roared past, oblivious to the foot traffic or the speed limit. One of the several gathered sheriff's vehicles began to give chase.

Judy stared, mute. She had no need to read body language to know that these people were up to no good, and Bryce's angst seemed to grow.

"Stay here, Judy. I think—"

The sky teemed with screaming blackbirds. Deep-throated gurgles of machine-gun fire made the baby behind Judy shrill. The young woman cursed and ran back into the building.

"Back, stay against the wall!" Bryce moved against the tide of running, frightened people. Open jeeps carrying about a dozen youth dressed in military-style camouflaged clothing, all toting shotguns and rifles, honked as they came into view from the north.

One man sporting a bandanna tied around his long greasy hair held up a bullhorn. "The Woodsmen need your attention!"

Judy pushed away from her shelter against the warm bricks to get a better look. They went past in a near blur as, one by one, squad cars flashed lights and sirens wailed. Only bits and pieces of the young man's speech warbled through the cacophony. Judy caught "land" and "trash" and "never give up." A final rifle blast echoed upon their exit from town.

Bryce loped back along the street. A few tourists began to straggle out from their cover under awnings. The drugstore and two gift shops disgorged more disgruntled customers. Bryce took Judy's arm. "I have the distinct impression we aren't going to be able to talk to any of those folk."

"I would agree." Judy took a deep breath. "No wonder the authorities want to catch and stop those people. They're dangerous. But I think I've figured out what they wanted to hide in the bomb shelter at my place. Hart and I couldn't tell what was in the crates, but as soon as we get back, I'm going to check them out. I bet they're full of guns and ammunition."

Bryce hurried her toward his car and held her door while she got in. He cleared his throat before they got underway. "I think I'll rest at that truck stop on the freeway down a few miles."

"Are you all right, Bryce? Do you want me to drive?"

"Thank you, but I'm fine. Just not as young as I used to be."

The truck stop was a large complex that included a restaurant, motel, and gift shop besides gas pumps. Bryce said he'd be right back, so she decided to wait outside for him. She considered her next move, alternately pacing and staring in the distance. When she came back to the present, her eyes lit on a strangely familiar truck. Too far away to read the plate, Judy glanced at the door of the truck stop to see if Bryce was headed back. She moved closer to take a look and was rewarded with a correct guess. *Now, why is Hart's truck here?* Scanning the parking lot didn't help. She affected a nonchalant saunter toward the restaurant, keeping an eye out for Bryce.

Judy scanned the patrons visible through the diner's windows. The fourth window was in shadow. Annoyed now, she quit pussyfooting and stomped through the front door, one loose shoelace flapping around her ankle, threatening to trip her. She didn't stop.

The back of Hart's head showed over one of the maroon booths. Hart! It was definitely him. Judy's heart sped. But who was the gorgeous, tanned blond who sat across from him, waving around a sparkly ring, laughing and obviously enraptured by her companion's company? *Nobody I've ever met.*

17

Judy charged headlong toward the restaurant's door and smacked directly into a waitress with a tray of sandwiches and drinks. She didn't stop to think about how many shades of red shone in the fever on her face and shoulders, but she was sure Hart had seen her. One sneaker stuck in the gooey salad mess on the floor. Judy ran right out of the loose shoe and left it there.

Bryce stood in the lobby, holding the door open for a slow-moving patron. Judy waved, biting her lip and barely slowing down. "Let's just leave, Bryce. Go home!"

If Bryce was surprised to see her come limping in a fast trot from the restaurant, he asked no questions.

Judy jumped into Bryce's car and huddled against the seat, too shaken to explain to Bryce what she'd seen. She closed her eyes, reviewing the scenario—Hart's hand had touched the other woman's across the table. She was sure she'd seen that intimate gesture. Still, Hart didn't seem the type who would lie so outrageously. Judy brought her fingers to her lips. Something else about the scene. The woman bore no resemblance at all to Hart. And the way she'd looked at him! As if he was the meal. Still. . .

After several minutes of contemplation, Judy ventured a question. "Bryce?"

"Are you ready to talk, Judy? What upset you?"

"I may have. . . I don't know. I. . .saw. . .someone.

Does. . .do you know if Hart has a sister?"

"I believe so. Quite a bit older than he."

"So not a gorgeous blond?"

"Well, I'm sure her husband thinks she's gorgeous. And to me she'd be young. I'm sorry, my dear, but I honestly don't know if she's blond."

"I doubt it." The mumble came out under her breath.

"What's that? I didn't hear you. That semi just passing was loud."

"I saw Hart back there. In the restaurant."

"Oh. I wondered if one of those trucks didn't look like his. And I take it you saw him with a woman."

"Yes." The other nagging twinge of information came back. "She looked like she had on camouflage clothing, like those KOWPIE people."

"Judy, how could one of them have gotten to this truck stop so quickly? With the police looking for them?"

"I guess you're right."

He glanced her way again, kindly laughter in his eyes. "I take it you're not a woman who cares much for shoes in pairs."

Judy looked down at her one bare foot, groaned, and flopped back against the seat.

Bryce drove the rest of the way without any other stops. When he pulled into her driveway and cut the engine, Judy fumbled with the latch on her seat belt. "I don't think your lost gold had anything to do with why Louise died. I admit you were on my list of suspects for a very short time, and only because of the gold. But it's ridiculous you'd even consider anything so heinous. I can only think someone from KOWPIE wanted to hurt Louise, and I think I know why. Do you want to come and look in the bomb shelter with me? I'm sure Clyde had his men clear away the debris by now."

Bryce patted her hand. "Sure. Let's do that. You had a reason for suspecting me, of course, and I don't blame you. And for the record, we searched the shelter up and down for my gold after Louise confessed."

"Okay. I'll go get the lantern from the garage. Be right back." Judy made a stop in the mudroom for a pair of garden clogs. When she returned, she saw Bryce standing at the barnyard fence, staring into the yard.

"Bryce?" Judy approached him. "Is anything wrong?"

"Hart didn't move any cattle yet, did he?"

"He and Red just finished the gate at his place. He said he'd start taking the calves when he gets back." The Herefords stood in their red and white dignity. Something didn't seem right. She counted them.

"I only see nine. Where're the others?" Judy climbed the fence. Two of the cows watched her nervously from the corners of their eyes.

"Hey, take it easy," Judy said to the animals. "I'm just checking up. You ladies know who I am." She walked gingerly around them. "This is not your normal smell, girls. What have you been into?" Judy walked around the corner of the barn and stopped short. One of the beautiful animals sank to its knees, nose to the ground, mouth foaming. Another was down completely, tossing its head.

Bryce met up with her there. "You'd better call the vet."

By the time the middle-aged man arrived, dressed in his thigh-high rubber boots and stethoscope wrapped around his belt, two more of the cows had gone down. Dr. Collins stood for a long moment, observing, before wading in to examine them. Bryce helped by grabbing a head or holding a flailing hoof out of the way.

Judy waited anxiously.

The vet fired questions. "What's in their feed? What have you been giving them? Where's the water supply?"

"I'm sorry, I don't know," Judy said, feeling stupid. She apologized over and over for not being able to answer him. She could only give him the vaccination record and show him the bags of feed and hay bales.

The doctor just shook his head. "Without knowing anything more specific, all I can do is take some samples to see if we can figure out what we're dealing with here. I don't see anything unusual in their immediate surroundings that would warrant these symptoms. And I strongly recommend you pay more attention to their environment. Start with the water. Get a new hose and clean out the tanks and let them air dry, away from the herd. Or better yet, get new ones."

Hart's calves bawled from the lower level of the barn. Bryce studied them. "Didn't Red come in yet? I thought he was choring for Hart."

The vet examined the water trough and sniffed the feed. "Seems fresh." He straightened. "Miss Winters,

Bryce, I recommend you separate the unaffected cows for the time being. Is there an isolated place you can board them until we figure out what's going on?"

"Yes, there is. We'll do that right away." Judy thanked the doctor and walked him to his van.

Dr. Collins stored his gear and turned to shake her hand. "I'll get these samples to the lab right away. I'm sorry about all this. Puzzled, too. Wish I could have done more."

"I appreciate that you came so quickly, Doctor. I gave you my cell number, right?" He answered with a nod. Judy said, "Okay. We'll be in touch."

Bryce joined her in the driveway. "We'll need some help. I take it you want to move them to Hart's? Let's call Red and have him bring his loader. He needs to tell us what he did differently, if anything. I want to phone Ardyth, too."

Judy walked him into the house. "I just don't understand. What could have happened?"

"I don't know. I've never seen anything in the yard or the pasture that could have this affect. Of course, the fields have been fallow—no plowing or spraying for a while. Something could have blown in on the wind and taken root. We can drive around and look later."

Bryce made his calls. Red shouted up and down that he knew nothing, but of course he'd come right away and vowed to do anything to help. Ardyth was on her way.

"Should we call the sheriff, too? The cows were fine yesterday," Judy said to Bryce. "I don't know, but I've been looking over my shoulder all summer, waiting for something to happen." She couldn't settle down. One minute she had to be outside, the next she went to putter in the kitchen where Bryce waited with more patience.

Bryce gave her an awkward fatherly pat on the shoulder. The screen door banged. Ardyth streamed in, red-and-white-plaid hair ribbon flying behind her. Bryce went to take her elbow.

Red knocked at the door. "You folks ready?"

Ardyth jumped when Bryce hollered back, "Coming!"

Ardyth sniffed and set her purse on a chair. "Well, we'll put that worry under our hats for the time being. What can I do to help now?" The elderly woman was practical, no matter the crisis. "Knowing Bryce, he didn't stop for lunch. I'll fix something and have it ready for when you get back. Go on now." She bustled familiarly around the kitchen, sending out the sheriff's deputy when he arrived.

Judy caught up to the others in time to see Red back up to the fence. Bryce grabbed a prod from the barn and got to work.

The men loaded and moved the cows, settling them with a minimum of fuss. Bryce checked them over carefully before thanking Red. Judy added her gratitude. "I'm sure glad you and Hart got the fence and gate set, Red. Nice job."

Red bobbed his head. "We planned to get in that third crop of hay next week. Don't know what'll happen now." He checked the sky, as if the answer would be written up there. "Need dry weather. I'm real sorry,

Miss Judy, about all this. I don't know what could have happened. On my honor, I would never hurt the stock. It goes against all gentleman farmer ettyket."

Judy shook his gnarled hand. "Thank you, Red. I'm sure the tests Doc took will tell us what's wrong. I appreciate your help today."

Bryce waved off the deputy and Red.

"Bryce, I never said anything before, and I didn't think about it when Doc was here, but a couple of weeks ago Hart and I saw Carranza moving kittens from the barn. We never did see old Irma, the mother. Now I wonder if something happened to her. I never did ask, but you didn't set any poison out, did you? For rats or anything?"

"No." Bryce shook his head. "I wouldn't do that anyway, without asking you first. You didn't find anything else unusual?"

Judy gave a helpless shrug. She still had a lot to learn about what was usual or not around a farm. "The only thing left to do is explore that bomb shelter. I've put it off long enough, and Graham's not around to bother me anymore. Those boxes down there have to be some kind of clue to everything that's happening. Nothing's going to stop me from going in there when we get back to my place. I'm not afraid of what anyone thinks anymore." Judy gulped. "But will you join me?"

Judy led the way down the cement steps, lantern aloft.

Bryce had the crowbar and mallet. He easily popped

the lid off the first crate. Judy could see the gleam of the metal of firearms among the packing material. Bryce made a count of that crate then estimated the entire stash by the number of crates. Judy brought her camera and snapped a dozen photos. Bryce held the lantern for her. When she finished, he declared it was time to call in the authorities.

If Sheriff Danner had been surprised by Judy's second call following so closely upon the first, she couldn't read it over the airwaves.

"So we thought—Bryce and I—that you might like to come and check out the bomb shelter," Judy stammered when Danner only grunted in response to her initial theorizing about the KOWPIE group wanting Louise's farm to store their weapons.

"Let me get this straight. You and Edwards were up near Coon Junction. You saw some kind of shoot 'em up parade with those numskulls, and now you see guns down in your bomb shelter? And you think all those people want to take over your farm? And these same numskulls killed Louise? A case that I have closed to my satisfaction? Hang on a minute; I have a message."

Judy rolled her eyes in Bryce's direction. "He's looking at another message, and he doesn't sound like he believes me."

"Miss Winters?" Sheriff Danner's gravelly voice came over the phone. "You and Mr. Edwards stay right where you are. Don't touch anything. We'll be right out."

At this, Judy held the phone away from her ear and frowned. "Now he says he's coming right over. I don't get it."

"He'll let us know when he gets here. In the meantime, can you show me more about that camera? I've heard about those digital things."

Judy heard the sirens long before three squads roared into the driveway. She exchanged a curious look with Bryce. Several uniformed officers swarmed over the yard. Judy and Bryce backed up while three of them clattered into the shelter.

"Sorry, folks," Danner said when he got within talking distance. "Don't mean to alarm you. The Federal Bureau of Alcohol, Tobacco, Firearms, and Explosives folk will be joining us shortly."

Judy put her hands on her hips. "What's going on, Sheriff?"

"Doc Collins called me. He got the initial lab screening from your cattle already."

Bryce stuck out his chin. "What did he find?"

"Ricin. Collins wanted to let me know immediately. He thought it was so odd and just read in one of his journals about cows getting into it down south. Since nothing like that grows around here, he assumed it was a deliberate act."

Judy's mind began to go fuzzy with weariness. "Ricin is a plant? I thought it was a gas."

Bryce smacked his forehead. "I can't believe it. Ricin is the byproduct of castor beans. The oil is the only part of the plant that's safe. Everything else about it is poisonous. In fact, Sheriff, haven't we heard ricin called the assassin's poison?"

Bryce had stolen Danner's thunder. "Yeah, that's right."

"Graham Montgomery knows about it," Judy said, the fuzziness evaporating in an onslaught of anger. "That's the plant he gave to Louise. It was right there, in the dining room. Graham talks about poisons all the time, even wears a necklace of bean seeds, like the ones Carranza was playing with! When Hart saw it, he told me it was dangerous and took the plant away."

Danner took notes. "Hart Wingate wears a necklace of castor beans?"

"No, no. Graham does."

Danner fixed her with a determined stare. "Who's Graham?"

"Graham Montgomery. He's a teacher in Lewiston. I used to go out with him. He came to see Aunt Louise. He said he had business here. Carranza hates him. Oh, and he wears fatigues all the time."

Danner scribbled and crossed out his markings then scribbled some more. "Let me get this straight. . . . Who's Carran— What was that?"

Bryce took over at that point, talking quietly and explaining about Graham Montgomery, Hart, and Carranza, while Judy watched the activity around the shelter. Several crates were stacked in the glare of the headlights. One of the officers approached their group. "Sheriff? Agent Markov from the Madison ATF Bureau is on the line."

"Excuse me, folks."

Judy didn't keep track of how much time passed before papers were thrust in front of her face with an attached pen. Bryce urged her to sign so the authorities could take away the crates. When the last of the official vehicles left the yard, all Judy could think about was how she could smooth the rut marks left in the grass.

Bryce urged her to go inside. "Come on, Judy. They're all gone. I closed the bomb shelter door."

Judy followed him, swaying in her exhaustion. "It's been a long day, Bryce. If I'm this tired, you have to feel worse. You drove, too, and helped with the cows. The poor cows."

"I'm not arguing, Judy. Here now, you'd better go home with Ardyth."

"Thanks, but I'm not leaving the animals alone."

Bryce frowned. "Stubborn. All right, then, lock up tight. I'll call you in the morning. We have to go to the station and give our statements."

"Okay. Did they find Graham?"

"I don't know. Go to bed. We'll talk about this in the morning. Lock the door behind me."

Judy dreamed of cows wearing necklaces and sunglasses. They laughed when she shone a flashlight on them. A bigger light blinded her, fading away to reveal Graham sitting on a high mountain of crates filled with guns. Aunt Louise stood at the base of the mountain, trying to tell him something.

18

J udy woke the next morning, her dream a tattered
memory. She and Bryce visited Sheriff Danner and
the ATF agent, again telling their stories. She gave them
all the details she knew about Graham Montgomery and
his tales of poison. She promised to turn over the remains
of the castor bean plant as soon as she found it.

The rest of the day passed in agonizing slowness.
She, Bryce, and Dr. Collins checked the remaining
cattle. They all searched the entire barn again for any
sign of ricin. Tucked away under a crumbling section
of the ramp to the upper barn was the stiff body of the
mother cat. Trampled along the edge of the barn were
a few fragments of what could have been castor beans.
The sheriff's deputies and a detective came out once
again, taking pictures and measurements and asking
questions for which Judy had no answers.

By evening, Judy huddled in misery on the front
porch swing in the gauzy mauve of twilight. The swing
groaned as she idly pushed on the floor with her foot.

Hart pulled into the driveway and stopped. He
rested his hands on the steering wheel of the pickup,
watching the house for several moments before he
opened the door and trudged toward her back door,
holding something in his hand.

Judy thought she was safely hidden on the porch
swing. She ducked her head to rest on the cushion
and kept watch from under the fringe of the afghan

she'd brought out. A mosquito whined near her ear. She gave it an abbreviated jerky wave. Hart was out of her view now. Judy held her breath, waiting. She heard him knock. *Maybe he'd just go away.*

Hart moved from behind the house, past his truck, and across the driveway toward the empty pasture. *Drat! Couldn't he just go away?* He set his elbows on top of the fence post and faced the setting sun. The mosquitoes were getting worse, and Judy pulled the afghan around her ears. But then she couldn't see well.

She flapped the blanket, brushing away the bloodsuckers. Hart bowed his head as he stood. Judy drew in a ragged breath, determined to hold onto her disappointment. *Leave. Leave.* If she chanted, would it happen?

He squared his shoulders, nodded once, and turned around again. He strode, head held high, to her back door. She heard him batter at the door and call her name. She started the swing.

Creak, creak, creak.

Swallows flitted through the evening air, doing their part to keep the mosquito population down. Crickets stopped while a lone frog began a lonely dirge. Judy stared at the porch floor in stony woe. She heard him come up the steps. Her eyes spilled over.

"Judy." Hart crouched in front of the swing, whispering near her nose. He reached out a hand, hesitated, and then settled his long fingers on the side of her face. "Judy, please. Look at me."

"We're just neighbors, Hart. You're leaving soon to go back to school. I saw your beautiful girlfriend. Congratulations."

Hart let his breath out. His hand continued to stroke her face. He brushed a mosquito away. She heard him take another quick breath. "Being neighbors isn't a bad thing. It's how we met. Didn't you get my message? I'm hoping to stay around, do most of the project work online for school." His fingers brushed at her tears.

Judy opened her eyes to see him hold up her lost sneaker. "I do think you're beautiful. We haven't talked about it yet, but I've come to hope that someday the owner of this shoe will have me for her husband."

Judy raised her eyes from the shoe to his lips. She sniffed and dared to look him in the eyes. "Polygamy is illegal in this state."

"When Amber called me at home, I agreed to meet her. She wanted to tell me about her new husband. We talked. I needed to hear her out, put our relationship to rest. She called out of the blue. I didn't have time to tell you or I would have. If I'd known you were there, which, by the way, you need to explain, I would have asked you to come, too."

Judy turned the screws. "Eight cows died. You weren't here."

"I know. I'm so sorry. The police just left. In fact, it's been a long evening."

"I bet."

"Judy." Hart stared off at the horizon. "I don't know why it didn't occur to me about that Montgomery guy using the poison plant to hurt Louise. Sheriff Danner said they'd tried to take him in for questioning but couldn't find him yet. On top of the Amber thing, the cows. . . I only took off for a few days. Do you people just have to save it up for when I'm gone, or what?"

Judy couldn't halt the stream of tears. Once unleashed, the dam poured over. Pent-up emotion, the life change she'd made, the deaths of the animals, her aunt's death. . .all of it erupted.

"Judy, please." Hart drew her from the swing onto the floor, rocking her. "Everything will work out."

"So—so many things—are—happening all at once. I just can't deal with it."

"Okay. Let's get you inside." Hart helped her up and took her into the house. They settled on the couch, and Judy cried herself out until she slept.

19

Judy awoke to find Hart watching her from the wing chair. He'd turned on a lamp and covered her with one of Una's bright afghans. She held out a hand and he came straight over, never taking his eyes off her.

Judy cleared her throat. "I haven't been sleeping well." She drew a shaky breath.

"Can you forgive me?" Hart asked.

"I don't know that it's my place to do that," Judy said, watching the interplay of their fingers in the soft, glowing light.

"Pastor Tyson said that you should ask forgiveness of anyone you've wounded by word or deed or even thought. I've hurt you, and so I ask your forgiveness."

Judy saw the golden flecks in his eyes, the sincerity of his words. "I forgive you, Hart. I said some pretty mean things to you, too. Will you forgive me?"

He closed his eyes and bent his head, bringing their entwined hands to his cheek.

"Forgiven. Forgotten. About not being here when you needed me. . .well, sometimes that happens. I'm not always in control of every circumstance. And it might be that sometimes you'll be away when I need you."

Judy nodded. "Okay."

He hesitated before raising his head again. "After Bryce talked me into going to Bible study with him, I started talking to Pastor Tyson about matters of faith.

I just assumed that going to church, trying to be kind, helping out people—that kind of thing, was enough. Then you came into my life. I watched how you spoke, acted, prayed about decisions you had to make, even when we weren't at church. You made me realize that faith was more than just doing what you thought was the right thing. Your faith is real. I always thought that being good was the way to heaven."

Hart made a rueful expression with his mouth. He turned her hand over and traced his finger along her palm. Judy stayed quiet, waiting until he spoke again.

"Last year, Pastor Tyson showed me this passage in the Bible about believing in Jesus but also receiving Him into your life. No one ever said anything like that to me before—at least, I never heard it. So, that's what he helped me do—receive Him."

Hart looked into her eyes, as if he could will her into seeing what he had come to know. She felt a little of the awe, the joy, he shared. Hart smiled, the flecks around his irises pulsing, holding Judy mesmerized. "I started reading my Bible, not only for a Bible study lesson, but to learn God's ways. Have you ever done that?"

Judy slowly nodded over their grasped hands.

"In the first book, Matthew, I get to this place where it says—" Hart closed his eyes to recite: " 'Do not store up for yourselves treasures on earth, where moth and rust destroy, and where thieves break in and steal. But store up for yourselves treasures in heaven, where moth and rust do not destroy, and where thieves do not break in and steal.' "

He opened his eyes and looked at her. "Now, here's the cool part: 'For where your treasure is, there your heart will be also.' I know this next idea is the corniest thing ever, but I was thinking about it, and it seems like our story—you know, was like looking for Bryce's lost treasure. Only, when he lost his heart, his one true love, he didn't care about his treasure anymore."

His face began to darken and he squeezed her hand. "And then I was thinking more, and it seemed like maybe it meant me, you know. 'Hart' for 'heart.' I want to be here for you as much as I can. I want to be your treasure. I know Jesus isn't talking about gold but about faith. I thought maybe we could practice that together."

"I'm still asleep, right? Pinch me!"

Hart laughed and gathered her up in a bear hug. "No, you're not dreaming. After I got home and found out about the cows and what you had going on over here, my world crashed. I wondered if there could be anything between us. But after tonight—"

"It took a lot of courage to come here."

"More than that. I had faith and hope. . .and love."

20

On Labor Day weekend, Judy had Bryce, Ardyth, and Hart over for dinner. Hart had helped with the meal preparation as he promised. Judy watched him measure rice and seasonings carefully and baste the turkey breast while privately thinking he fussed just a bit too much. He let her chop vegetables for the salad while he shook up flavored vinegar and oil for a dressing.

After dinner the four of them sat in the living room

"So, Judy, tell us about your new job," Ardyth said.

"It's just a school-year contract, to cover a leave of absence. Fifth grade."

Bryce reached for his coffee cup. "You taught eighth grade before, didn't you? This will be quite different."

"I've already met with Jane, my co-teacher. There are only the two fifth-grade classes, and we've decided to team-teach both rooms of students. That way we can both focus on our individual strengths. Everyone seems great, so far."

Ardyth wiggled under Bryce's arm, which he'd settled about her shoulders. "Was it hard to quit your former job?"

"There were good things and bad things about it," Judy said. She looked at Hart.

Carranza wandered in, stopping to rub against

Ardyth's ankles. She put a hand down to pat his head. "Is there any news about that other man who used to call on you?"

Hart and Bryce shook their heads. "Not yet. They'll find him," Bryce said.

Judy hunched her shoulders and shivered. "I feel so weird. And creepy, and sad. In the back of my mind I had questions about him. I still have a hard time believing he was just using me to get to Aunt Louise. And that he'd commit murder."

Hart pulled her close and kissed the top of her head.

"Well, at least you two seem to have hit it off." Ardyth smiled. "I can't imagine a nicer couple."

Judy felt her face go hot. She rubbed her cheek against Hart's shoulder.

"Ahem. So, Hart, what news from home?" Bryce asked.

"Oh, my parents are fine. The farm's running better than ever, with milk prices up now."

"Hart's got two courses scheduled over the Internet for fall," Judy added.

Ardyth gasped. "What? By computer, you mean? You can do that? That's wonderful. Bryce tells me that you're following in his footsteps in engineering school."

Hart's grin went from ear to ear, as it was Bryce's turn to blush.

"Yep. Bryce took me under his wing, I guess you could say." Hart laughed.

"I think it's wonderful." Judy gave Hart's arm a shake.

"Almost as wonderful as nurturing the minds of America's children," Hart murmured.

Ardyth clapped her palms against her lap. "Well, enough of this lovefest for me, kids. I want to get home. Bryce?"

With a frantic look at Hart, Judy rose. "Can you wait a minute, Ardyth? We—Hart and I—have something we want to show the two of you. Together."

Hart went to pick up the yellowed envelope from the table Judy kept near the staircase. Together they held the faded rectangle in front of the older couple.

Bryce whistled through his teeth: the schoolboy kind of sound of a bomb falling and exploding.

Ardyth put a hand to her mouth. "Oh dear." She squinted. "What's the date?"

Bryce held out a steady hand and took the letter. "I suppose Harold set this aside and forgot all about it in the excitement of getting home and his wedding. Where did you find it?"

"Behind the floorboard in the closet of my room," Judy said.

"When we were replacing the wall," Hart added.

Ardyth reached for it, but Bryce held the envelope away. "I don't know if I'm ready to give you this yet, my dear."

"But you addressed it to me."

Judy leaned back into Hart's embrace. "We had that same struggle. That's why we agreed to show both of you together."

Bryce said, "Ardyth, please. Will you trust me just a little longer? I promise that someday I will show this to you."

Ardyth's silver head bobbed once, her faded eyes locked on Bryce's.

Bryce held out his hand. "You must understand. This is not just water under the bridge. This is fifty years of misunderstanding. We can't just undo all that in one evening."

Ardyth slipped her hand into his. "I trust you. I was there, remember? It was because I thought you didn't care that I went to school in Milwaukee." She turned to look at Judy and Hart. "I never returned another letter from Bryce."

Bryce took up the narrative. "I had to go on—learn how to make a living. Anyone could see that farming the small home place was going the way of the dodo bird."

Hart and Judy shared a rueful glance.

"I was traipsing all over the country, showing off my fancy equipment, doing training seminars."

"You two didn't talk?" Hart asked.

"Love can be dumb, like a rock, I guess," Bryce said. "I figured Ardyth couldn't want a fella like me. Familiarity breeds contempt, you know."

"Then I moved away to St. Louis," Ardyth concluded.

No one followed the steps through the next decades. Ardyth had her memories, her family. Bryce had his career.

After Ardyth and Bryce left, Hart helped clean up.

"I wonder how long Bryce will make Ardyth wait to read that letter," Judy said.

Hart tilted his head. "I think he has other reasons than just words."

"Like the gold? He said the gold didn't matter to

him if Ardyth didn't share his life."

"And now they're together."

"I can't imagine how Bryce went fifty years loving Ardyth even though she married someone else."

Hart trailed his fingers along her cheeks. "I can."

—

By the end of September, Judy had worked out a flexible classroom routine. She spent her first week teaching at Robertsville Elementary learning how to talk to ten- and eleven-year-olds. They weren't the teenagers Judy had been used to dealing with and had a different vocabulary. Robertsville ran a middle school of sixth, seventh, and eighth graders, and these fifth grade students knew they were kings of the heap for at least this year.

Summer rains came late. Sticky September weather made everyone a little cranky. Judy was certain she had seen an old box fan in the attic the last time she had been up there. Her room at school was hot, and the fan would help.

Late on a Sunday afternoon, she pulled down the creaky steps, carrying a portable lantern at shoulder height. Shadows leapt out at her as she pivoted, searching. Aunt Louise's dollhouse seemed to beckon. Judy set the lantern nearby and pulled off the dustcover. The Porters, Mr. and Mrs., with their littlest girl Priscilla, waved to her from their house. Fan forgotten, Judy set about rearranging their furniture and repositioning the family.

She heard a *bang* downstairs and jumped. Judy grabbed the lantern and tiptoed across the beams to the stairs. She listened, holding her breath.

"Judy! Judy! Where are you?"

Judy let out the breath. "I'm up here, Hart," she called. "In the attic."

He came pounding upstairs.

"No wonder you didn't hear me knock. And you should keep the door locked. What are you doing?" His head came up through the entrance. He hauled himself up and sat on the edge.

"Hi!"

"Hi, yourself," Judy said. "Hey, I'd like you to meet some old friends, the Porters."

Hart cocked his head, obviously questioning her sanity.

Judy laughed and beckoned him over to the dollhouse. Hart followed.

"Ah, I see."

"Mr. and Mrs. Porter, this is Hart. He's a special pal of mine. Hart, this is Mr. and Mrs. Porter and their daughters Polly and Priscilla."

"Tell me they have a dog."

"Of course." Judy held up the tiny toy poodle. "Meet Poindexter."

"You're kidding."

Judy noticed his reverent touch of the beautiful details on the framework. "Uncle Harold made this for Louise when she was little."

"Wow. You should have this downstairs. Mice or something might get at it up here."

"I'm considering it."

"So, this is what you were doing? Playing with dolls?"

"Well, that and looking for a fan. I thought I saw one up here once. A big old box type."

"Oh?"

"My room at school's really warm, and the screen has a big hole. The maintenance guy said they weren't going to get to it this year. So I thought a fan would help."

"Can't they get a fan for you?"

Judy gave him a withering stare. "Of course *they* can't. *They* is you and me, pardner. We taxpayers. And we taxpayers don't give enough for incidentals like fans." Judy shook her head. "You've got a lot to learn about the life of a public service provider."

Hart hauled her into a hug. "Mm, you're right. So let's get started."

She reveled in the tenderness Hart showed her. Their kisses were deep and precious. "I think this is private service, Hart," she said breathlessly.

"You could be right." He gulped the dusty air and closed his eyes. "Someday."

"Yes, someday," Judy agreed, caressing his arms.

"So, where's this fan?"

"I was too busy playing to find it. Help me look."

"Hold the lantern over here."

"Oh—I think I see it. There, Hart, under the eaves."

They stepped around odds and ends, boxes of canning jars, a birdcage, and a case of warped vinyl record albums gathering dust.

Hart swung the lantern around.

"Hey, hold still. Moving the lantern like that makes the shadows seem alive. I'm getting the creeps." Together they hauled at the fan until they got it away from the wall. Hart checked the cord.

"Hmm, looks okay. We'll try it out downstairs."

"Hart, look at this," Judy squatted near a dark shape that had been hidden behind the fan.

"What do you see?"

"It looks like an old trunk." Judy tugged. "It's stuck. Help me." She feared the leather handles were too fragile to handle it roughly.

"How old do you think that thing is?"

"I have no idea," Judy said. "It's really jammed in back there."

"All of this humidity must be making the timbers swell around it. I think we need something to pry at it with or something. Hey! A crowbar. Didn't we put one back in the garage after we fixed the closet? I'll just run down and see."

"Why don't you let me, Hart? I could use a stretch."

"Okay. I think I hung it on the tool bench Peg-Board, back behind your aunt's old car."

"I'll be right back." Judy smiled as she went down the steps. "Don't go anywhere. And I'll know if you toyed with Poindexter."

Hart groaned. "Yeah, right."

Judy stopped to pick up the torch flashlight by the back door. A new moon meant little light outside.

The remaining cattle were in Hart's possession. The barnyard was silent. Judy made her way over to the garage, using the flashlight to guide her. She stopped at the side door and listened.

A humid gust rattled the maple in the yard every now and then. The lilac bushes rustled. Judy turned the flashlight off and stood still.

The out-of-sync rustling sounded again. Judy slipped around the edge of the garage, straining to see in the blackness. A light from the front porch sent a beam across the yard, illuminating the shadow creeping along the fence.

Sweat beaded along her spine. Heart pounding, she crept back into the house and up the stairs.

"Hart," Judy whispered as loudly as she could into the stairwell that led up to the attic.

He thrust his head through the attic door. "What?" He stage-whispered back. When he noticed her shiver, he immediately swung down. "What's the matter?"

"There's someone out there. I don't know if he saw me or not."

Judy rubbed at the goose bumps on her arms. Hart watched her, a worry line between his dark brows.

"Call the emergency number, okay?" Hart said as he pushed himself down the attic stairs. "I'll go out and see what's up. It might just be somebody lost or a stray dog or something. You're sure what you saw was big enough to be a person?"

Judy just nodded, her teeth chattering. Hart's eyes darkened.

"Okay. Let's go. I'm sure there's nothing serious."

Judy watched outside the door for a few seconds. She went back inside to call the police. As she stood again at the door, listening to the wind rise, she decided to turn on the garage light. The light revealed the back of a little blue car. Graham's.

There! Judy squinted in the dark, willing her eyes to pick out details through the screen. A shout! Who was it? Judy grabbed the first hard object she came in contact with, a leftover piece of two-by-four, and headed out the door.

At the lower level of the barn she stopped at the sound of the voices of Hart and another man.

"Oof—hey!"

"What are you doing? Who are you and what do you want?"

An answering slap of flesh on flesh made Judy's stomach churn. She didn't dare distract Hart. But what could she do? She peered through the door and drew in a quick, shaky huff when a body came hurtling through the empty lower level of the barn, followed by another, diving on top of the first.

"You—I'll teach you to mess with me." Judy recognized Graham's voice. He grunted. She could hear Hart gasping.

She reached through the door and turned on the overhead flood. Graham stretched full length over Hart, hands wrapped around his victim's throat. Graham hissed and growled maniacally, while Hart tried to bring his knees up and claw the other man's hands away.

"Graham!" Judy started toward them.

Graham turned his head in her direction. She barely recognized his face, it was so distorted with rage. One eye swelled, and blood dripped from his nose. Hart struggled to keep his face from direct splatters.

"Graham!" Judy could see Hart losing ground. "What are you doing? Get away from here!"

Graham screamed curses in reply.

A feline shriek and growl added to the din. Carranza streaked by, flying onto Graham's exposed neck. This time Graham did not cry out for Judy to help him. While pinning Hart's shoulders with his knees, Graham reached behind him and savagely twisted the cat from his shirt. He shook Carranza hard and hurled the body into the black of the yard.

With little time to take in the shocking turn of events, Judy watched Hart's face begin to darken and swell as Graham tightened his choke hold on Hart.

Choking wasn't Hart's only danger. Graham's menacing black necklace hung scant millimeters above Hart's mouth.

"You remember this, my dear Judy, don't you? These lovely beads."

If only she could distract him long enough for Hart to get a second wind. "Graham, why are you here? What are you doing?"

"You cost me my lifework." He vented his fury on Hart's throat, shaking him.

"You mean KOWPIE, don't you?" Judy had to get to him somehow. "The Woodsmen?"

"You cut me out of this place. It was a perfect setup for our operation. I spent years wooing that old woman into selling. Then you came along. I thought you just needed a little persuading. Even after, when I heard about the gold bonus! Who'd have imagined a fortune in gold? These precious castor beans will leave no trace, don't worry. No one will ever know what happened here. One pod has enough poison to kill several people. He only needs to chew one—just—a little." Graham lowered the necklace until a seed touched Hart's lips. "Like that stupid cat. Those idiot cows. And dear Louise."

Judy closed her eyes. He'd admitted to killing Louise. His voice went on with deadly intent. "In a few hours you'll begin to feel hot, burning all down your throat and into your stomach," he taunted Hart. "You'll have cramps and then convulsions."

Graham twisted his face toward the last place he'd heard Judy's voice. "There is no cure, no antidote. You're in agony every second until you die."

His grip slackened. "Judy? Where did you go? You need to see this. You have to be here to watch what—"

Judy swung the piece of two-by-four as hard as she could across his face.

She watched as the force of her blow flung him away from Hart. Graham heaped into a ball, shrieking. Judy bent over Hart, sobbing and shaking. He gripped her wrist while air whistled down his bruised throat.

A squad car, lights flashing red, pulled into the yard. Judy stood to wave them over.

She could hear the radio chatter in the background. Officers rushed into the circle of light. "Miss? Judy?

What's going on here?"

"Graham Montgomery attacked Hart Wingate. Graham's the one the sheriff has been looking for." Hart sat up, head bent. One of the officers knelt down beside them.

"Are you all right, sir? Ron! Call for an ambulance."

"No," Hart rasped. "Not for me."

"We need backup anyway," the officer said and made the call.

Graham began to wriggle as he lay on the ground. The officer reached for him.

"Be careful," Judy warned. "That necklace—just watch out. Don't touch any part of the beads. They're poison. Graham admitted to being with the environmental terrorists who left the weapons in my bomb shelter. And killing Louise and the cattle."

"From a necklace?"

"Those seeds are from the castor bean plant," Judy told them.

"Also known as ricin," Hart said, rasping. "A deadly toxin. I learned that in a class." He shook his head. Judy helped him get to his feet. "The poison metabolizes completely after time, leaving no trace. That's why they couldn't find it in Louise. The vet was able to test the cows quickly enough."

"Graham wanted Louise to give him this farm as their headquarters. When she realized what he was up to and tried to change her will, he killed her."

Graham struggled against the handcuffs. "You'll never pin that on me! You people don't understand. You have to be stopped. Everyone has to stop the insanity.

The government cannot be allowed to destroy nature. The only way you understand is by force. We humans do not have to follow your rules. You people have to respect nature. You can't waste water with flushing toilets and great big bathtubs. You know why I had to stop that guy you hired from his dangerous plot. We Woodsmen are bound to follow nature's order. Don't look at her! She'll read your mind."

Judy turned her back on his ravings. She watched Hart carefully. He gave her a weak smile and brought her ear to his mouth. "Check Carr—" He couldn't finish, but she knew what he meant. She got up to walk in the direction she'd seen Graham throw the cat. Too dark away from the yard lights to see, she soon returned to Hart, shaking her head.

Another squad, sirens blaring, pulled in, closely followed by Robertsville's ambulance.

"This way." One of the policemen guided the medics over to their group. One of them began to examine Hart's throat. "Wingate—we meet again. This is getting to be a bad habit. How're those ribs?"

"Tisk-tisk," the other medic beside Graham said. "Somebody did not qualify for their final dentist's exam. What a mess. Sir, did you swallow any teeth? Whoa! None of that. We need a spit mask here."

"Yeah, and be careful of those seed things around his neck. Folks here claim they're poison," the uniformed officer said.

"You don't say," his partner replied. "Can we get your statements, folks?"

By mid–October, the oak leaves had flamed out. The days grew shorter and chillier. Hart suffered no ill effects from his brush with the ricin.

Graham's lawyer worked on his insanity plea. Judy had little doubt he'd either end up in prison or an asylum.

Carranza had not come back nor did they find his remains.

Hart rested on the sofa in his own living room, head pillowed on Judy's lap, her left hand clasped in both of his. He whispered with his sore throat. "Poor Carranza. He deserved better."

Judy stroked the hair off his forehead. "I don't think I ever told you that Carranza belonged to me. I found him as a stray in Lewiston. When I rented an apartment, I couldn't have pets. Louise had moved to the farm, so she took him. I don't think he really forgave me for giving him away."

Hart squeezed her fingers. "I think he did. Look how he tried to warn you. And he protected his children." Hart swallowed. "Judy, what did that guy mean when he said you could read minds? Or was he crazy?"

Judy continued the rhythm of her touch. "I took a class once on how to interpret body language. I got pretty good at it."

"Ah. Sometimes I wondered about that myself.

My family wants to meet you," Hart reminded her in his raspy voice.

"I want to meet them, too. You know I don't have any time off, though, until Thanksgiving."

"It's a date."

Judy touched the fading bruises around Hart's neck.

"I guess we're about even," Hart said and released her hands to pull her head to his.

"But I fell on you twice." Judy had a hard time getting the words out while Hart nuzzled her lips.

"Yes, well, you couldn't have fallen on me in the bomb shelter if you hadn't found it first." He let her up for air. "Who knows where we'd be if the tornado had taken us for a ride."

"Emerald City?"

"At least."

"Robertsville is just fine, thank you," Judy said, kissing him back.

"Yes, let's keep saving each other's lives in Robertsville."

"Hah."

"And I think I'll sign us up for next summer's softball league. I hope you run half as well as you bat."

Gene Reynolds called during the aftermath of Graham's arrest. "So, that was quite the excitement out there at your place, I hear. I just want you to know that if you need my services as council, I am here for you."

"Thank you. That's very kind of you." Judy hung

up and made a face at the telephone. He had not forgotten about the possible sale of the property and called at least once a month to confirm that she had not changed her mind.

With Louise's murder finally atoned for, Judy turned her attention to the mystery surrounding Bryce's lost gold. Even if she planned to keep the property, she still wanted to help her friend find his stash.

Judy continued to read through Louise's diaries, going back through the years. Teenaged Louise reminisced about her own mother, who had suffered and died from cancer. Louise was inspired to continue keeping diaries where her mother Una had left off. "Mthr clthes all gvn awy. Diaries saf in trnk. Atc." Apparently Harold had all of his wife's personal belongings given or stored away. Louise had saved the diaries and put them away in the attic.

During one of Hart's weekend seminars away at school, Judy came home from church determined to pull that old trunk away from the wall. A rainy Sunday afternoon, she'd had to defend her time alone at home from her well-meaning friends by turning down two dinner invitations after the service. She quickly ate a cold lunch, changed clothes, and went up to the attic.

"Okay. Diaries. Trunk. Attic. Make my time worth it." Judy swung the lantern around. "Aha—and there we left it on that fateful day. And I still need a crowbar."

Judy went downstairs, picked up an umbrella, and splashed out to the garage, where she found the crowbar.

Back in the attic, Judy strained to pry the trunk out from under the eaves, trying not to damage it. She wrapped a dust cloth around the sharp, curved end of the bar and coaxed the trunk inch by inch onto the main floor. She crouched in front of it: a square, wooden flat-topped rectangle in an unappealing moldering brown, unwilling to release its secrets.

She tapped around the rim like she would a sealed pickle jar, hoping to loosen the cover and sneezing at each puff of dust. She wrinkled her nose. The metal clasp made a high-pitched squeal as Judy pried at the lid, breaking a fingernail in the process.

"You'd better be worth the trouble," she scolded the trunk. Judy lifted the lid and let it fall back on protesting hinges.

The first item she lifted away was the filmy wedding veil and crown of dried flowers she had seen Una wear in her wedding picture. Aunt Louise had never married, so Aunt Una never passed it on. Netting crackled with age. Judy stroked it with reverence and then laid the veil carefully aside.

A few cardboard framed photographs lay underneath. Judy sifted through them, setting them aside to examine them later.

She lifted out the first tray of the trunk to reach the second section. Here were embroidered handkerchiefs and two pairs of gloves. Judy fit her hand inside one of the pairs, soft kid leather which came halfway up her arm. So delicate. She held her hand to her cheek. The glove smelled of cedar.

Warm hands closed around her shoulders.

"Hart!" Judy leaned back into his caress. He pressed his cold cheek against her warmer one. "I didn't hear you come in," she said.

"Looks like you were preoccupied. I missed you." He pulled himself into cross-legged comfort next to her and eyed the contents of the trunk.

"What have you got here? You started without me," he mock complained.

"Sorry. And I could have been having dinner at the Harrises, I'll have you know."

"Hmm, and what made you give up that treat?"

"Curiosity and an open afternoon. How was your seminar?"

"Very educational."

"Ha."

"Tell you more later. Right now I'd rather hear about this."

"I read in Aunt Louise's diaries that Una kept journals, too. Louise wrote that she put them in her mother's trunk, so I decided to look. I'm pretty sure this is Una's trunk, but it might not be her only one. So I just started sorting through this stuff, but I haven't found the diaries yet."

"Okay." Hart leaned on an elbow. "Carry on. I'll supervise."

Judy gave him a playful shove. She reached into the trunk for some papers. "Tell me more about your class while I'm sorting," she said, sifting through a few years' worth of school papers marked with a childish "Una Swedeborg."

"It went well. Everything's on track. My work is acceptable or better, according to Professor Jordan. We had no questions or problems, so we'll keep going. My parents have been appropriately reassured that I'm still alive and headed in the right direction." He hugged her shoulders. "They can't wait to meet you and are planning on us coming for Thanksgiving." He leaned over her shoulder and whispered in her ear, "There'll be a crowd."

"Good. After all my growing-up years with just Aunt Louise and me, I can't think of anything better."

"I'll ask you about that again afterward." He put his finger on the page Judy was studying. "Isn't that Una's name? She was pretty smart, it looks like."

"Looks like. Oh—here, check this out." Judy held up a packet of letters tied with a blue ribbon.

"Look at those stamps." Hart whistled.

"Letters from home. Hey—some are in Swedish. How're your language skills?"

"Nonexistent," Hart said. "Swedish is not a required subject."

"Not for me, either. I wonder if anyone around here knows Swedish."

"Let's keep looking in the trunk," Hart said, leaning over the edge.

Judy grinned at his enthusiasm. She clutched another handful of bits and pieces. "I think I just hit pay dirt. This appears to be a diary." She held it up for Hart to see.

Judy opened the faded paper cover carefully. Cracked along the edges, the booklet had all kinds of papers sticking out.

Judy put her finger on the date of the inside cover. "See—that's the summer Louise was five years old."

"I can barely read the writing."

"Here. Come closer to the lamp."

"You read it," Hart urged.

Judy gingerly turned a few pages. "Today Louise gave us quite a scare," Judy squinted at the faded handwriting while she read out loud. "I thought the door to the bomb shelter was much too hard for her to ever get open. What a funny little girl. Our friend Bryce has been called away. He will work out of state for six months. I don't know how Harold will do without him. They are closer than brothers, I think. It is good for my man to have such a friend. They go fishing; they give each other advice. And Bryce loves Louise so. That man should have his own children, fond as he is of them. Bryce sometimes forgets that our Louise is too young to understand him. Just a little girl."

Judy turned the page over, telling Hart, "I'm glad she didn't use the same shorthand code Louise did. Reading hers is an exercise in frustration."

She continued to read from the diary. "Louise claims Bryce gave her a very important job. He apparently put a package in her little hands to watch over while he was away. If he were here now, I'd wring his neck, even though my love for him is vast. Making a little one worry. Bah! We had word that Bryce wanted to sell his farm. Harold does not believe this. Jenny is leaving home at last. She tires of her anger and of waiting for Bryce to make amends for something only she understands she is angry about. Such pride the woman has."

Judy slipped the first page under the second and continued reading.

"All this made me worry about Louise's task. So I went back into the shelter, certain that was the reason she was in there—she wanted to hide. And there I find the little box. That Bryce! Again, I would wring his neck and fry him up. Maybe I take back what I thought earlier, that he would make a good father. No. I know it's true. I will say nothing to Harold. I think my man at one time would have married Jenny, if he could. Better he knows nothing about what his friend has done."

Judy turned over the page. She and Hart touched foreheads in a mutual caress before she finished reading.

"I took the box. There have been break-ins in the neighborhood. The Lumleys had all their silver and their new television set stolen just last night. The first place a thief would look was in our bomb shelter. Everyone knows. Harold and I talk of filling it in, now that there doesn't seem to be so much danger from Russians. Louise must not be allowed to play and get trapped or hurt. What to do about Bryce's box? I will dig a hole and bury it. Everyone knows treasure should be buried. And what better place than the oak? I dig underneath the friendship letters. Then we will know where to look when Bryce returns."

Hart touched Judy's face, wiping at the tears. "You cry more than anyone I've ever known," he told her, once again pulling her close.

He finished reading the last sentence for her. "Tomorrow I see the doctor again. The pain in my gut is no better."

"I never used to cry. It's just so sad," Judy said. "Right after this Una found out she had cancer. According to Aunt Louise she wasn't ever fully cured and suffered until she died. I never met her."

"Come on, let's go show Bryce what we found." Hart pulled Judy to her feet.

At Bryce's house in town, Hart put the book into his friend's hands. The old man held the brittle diary, his nose twitching. He looked up at her and Hart with soft, rheumy eyes.

"I think we'd better leave you to read that for yourself," Hart said.

Bryce said nothing as he settled into an armchair, and they let themselves out.

"I hope he doesn't worry himself sick over this," Judy told Hart when he stopped at her house.

He walked her to her back door. "It's been over fifty years. I believe he and Ardyth will work it out."

"But what if we dig under the stump and don't find anything?"

Hart pulled her close. "It was all a long time ago. I don't know what will happen." Judy felt the expansion of his chest as he breathed in deeply. She listened to the steady *thump* of his heart.

"This leaving you at the doorstep is getting old," Hart complained after a few minutes. Judy smiled and waved him off. Hart stood at the door of the truck, watching until she latched the door. She moved the curtain to see him turning around and driving away.

"I agree," she whispered.

⎯⎯

The phone shrilled by Judy's head the next morning. She checked the alarm. Six fifteen. She usually didn't get up until six thirty to get ready for work.

She yawned and reached a limp arm out to pick up the receiver, certain she knew the identity of her caller. Judy snuggled under the quilt while she answered. "Good morning, Bryce."

"I'm sorry, Judy. I know you have to get to work and all."

"I'm surprised you're not over here with a bulldozer already," Judy said and rolled over, putting her arm up over her eyes.

Bryce's chuckle sounded choked. He cleared his throat. "Ah, well, it's been fifty years. A few more hours won't change anything. When do you get home from school?"

"Bryce, you know you don't have to wait for me."

"I can't imagine doing this without you."

Judy sat up and hugged her knees. "Well, I don't know if *I* can stand it. I may call in sick."

"Now, don't do that. We'll wait."

"This will be the longest day I've ever spent at school, then. I'll be home by three forty-five."

"A quarter to four it is, then," Bryce said.

Judy was right. The day seemed eternal. Nothing in particular went wrong. Jimmy Lauders threw up and had to go home. Janette Flaherty scribbled on her latest boyfriend, Kent, whose mother had already complained that Kent was the target of bullying from the girls. Judy had to stay and spend twenty minutes on the telephone trying to calm her down after the kids left and before she could clean up after class. Her dashboard clock read three fifty-five when Judy pulled into her driveway.

Hart opened her car door for her and reached for her heavy schoolbag.

Bryce stood nearby, leaning on a shovel, the picture of patience.

"Hey, didn't I see you posing as a statue in the middle of town?" Judy asked Bryce.

"Ha, ha. Welcome home, Judy," Bryce said.

"I've never been so eagerly anticipated. Well, where're the photographers, the press? The cameras?"

Hart grabbed her hand and pulled her over to the oak stump after depositing her bag on the front porch. "It's just us, Judy. Come on!"

Bryce gave them his heartiest grin before selecting the place to set the point of the spade. He thrust in then went still.

"Bryce? What's the matter? Are you okay?" Judy stepped forward to touch his arm, and Hart moved to Bryce's other side.

"Bryce! You didn't hurt yourself, did you? Already?

Is it your back?"

"No, no. Not my back. My brain! Doofus, I am!" He thrust the shovel into Hart's hands. "Same thing I do, over and over—I just don't deserve to breathe air, I don't. How could I be such a moron now?" He strode to his car, streaming epithets of idiocy against himself. He slammed the car door, gunned the engine, and headed down the road.

Judy frowned. "Well, what's gotten into him? Did he decide he wanted the *Reporter* here after all?"

"It's a guy thing." Hart squeezed her arm. "I think I know what he's doing. He'll be back soon, but he needs some time alone to think."

"Then I'm going to change clothes and get something to drink. I'll just put my stuff away, okay?"

"Hey, in a minute." Hart hugged her. "How was your day?"

"Ooh, that sounds awfully like old married people talk."

"Mmm, maybe."

"I like it."

"Me, too. So, how was your day?" Hart accompanied her inside, holding her hand.

"Endless. One child was sick and I had to take him to the office. One of the girls wrote on a boy. . . . Don't laugh. These kids are serious!"

By the time Judy came to the kitchen, Hart had coffee ready. They took mugs out to the porch swing to watch for Bryce's return.

Sure enough, five minutes later Bryce came squealing back into the yard. He opened the door for his passenger, a disgruntled Ardyth Belters.

"Bryce! For crying out loud, I was at the beauty parlor," Ardyth complained. "Couldn't you have waited at least until my hair was dry?" She tied a chiffon scarf over her curlers as she trudged to the tree stump with him.

"There! All present and accounted for." Bryce took up the shovel again.

"What's going on?" Ardyth asked.

"Just watch. I'm going," Bryce said, sticking the shovel blade deeply into the soil, "to show you"—he pitched a load off to the side—"just what"—he dug in again—"all the fuss"—another toss—"has been about."

After a dozen or so thrusts into the ground, Bryce tapped gently on something. He gave them all a beatific smile. Ardyth had her hands stuck deep into the pockets of her trench coat and her chin tucked into her collar, feigning indifference. Judy gripped Hart's hand with white knuckles.

Bryce bent over slowly, slowly, and reached in through the tangle of roots. He retrieved an object not much bigger than the palm of his hand. Rotted canvas dropped away as he lifted the box. He brushed the thing off and brought it over to Ardyth.

"What's that?"

Bryce looked into her eyes. "For over sixty years, you are all I've ever thought about, all I've ever wanted, all I've needed. Even when you thought you hated me, I still dreamed of having you at my side."

Ardyth opened her mouth then closed it. Her whole face puckered into a mass of confusion.

Hart wrapped his arms around Judy's waist.

"These folks found something that belonged to you awhile back. That letter I wrote you—my last letter before I came home from Alaska. For some reason which we'll never know, and which we'll forgive and forget about from this moment on, the letter was lost and never mentioned again. Here. It's yours." He took the faded envelope from his pocket and placed it into her hands.

"But first, I want you all to see this." He beckoned to Judy and Hart. "Come, everyone. Jenny, put that letter away." She did as she was told, for once without protest.

"Here, my dearest. I had these made, for you and me." He put the discolored little box into her hands. Together they opened it, eyes never leaving each other.

When Judy took in a noisy breath, Ardyth looked down.

"Oh." She reached into the box to touch it with a shaky forefinger. "Oh, my." Judy watched her shoulders slump.

"There was never any great wealth. Harold and I knew we weren't going to strike it rich. I thought you'd understand. We went for the adventure, not for tons of gold or to be playboys or any nonsense. I knew I wanted you for my wife even before we left. I always thought, if I could get enough gold—"

"You'd have rings made?" Ardyth asked.

"Wedding rings. Our wedding rings, my dear," Bryce said.

Judy felt the tears welling up and hid her face in Hart's shoulder. His hands soothed her back.

"This was your treasure all along?" Hart asked.

"Yes. This is it." He took the smaller of the rings from the box and held it up in the waning light. "See—here, I had our names engraved."

"Aw–awfully sure of yourself, w–weren't you?" Ardyth said.

"My whole world went up in smoke when you wouldn't even talk to me."

"I didn't know. How could I? Harold married for love. I didn't want your adventure to end with having you stuck with me. It would have meant that—"

"Even if there had been a bet, which there wasn't," Bryce said, "it would have meant that I was the winner. Don't you get it? *I* carved those letters. *I* was the one who wanted you. Harold didn't have anything to do with it. Here—read the letter."

Judy was barely able to speak. "Why don't you all come inside, where it's warmer and there's light? I'm sure you'll be more comfortable in the parlor."

Ardyth allowed herself to be handed into the house, where Hart and Judy left them alone.

"Wow." Hart lounged against the kitchen counter-top while watching Judy put together a tray of mugs and tea bags. "Even I have to admit that was fairly romantic."

Judy rolled her eyes at him, not ready to trust her voice.

"To think, all along, that's what he held on to, what was lost," Hart mused. "All those years, she was that precious to him that he couldn't ever marry anyone else."

"I don't think he ever stopped wondering what

became of the rings, even though he said he didn't care anymore after Ardyth moved away," Judy said.

"I wonder how Harold got mixed up in this."

"He must have felt terrible when he realized that he'd lost that letter."

Hart added the sugar bowl to the tray. "I wonder if Harold or Louise ever read Una's diary. I bet Louise did. Why didn't she say anything if she knew where the gold ended up?"

"I can't imagine keeping a secret like that. Do you think it's been long enough? Here, you take the tray."

A few weeks later Hart and Judy stood up with Bryce and Ardyth at their marriage ceremony.

Hart and Judy faced each other on either side of the altar. The burning candles made the atmosphere intimate, cozy. Hart's eyes were so solemn, so sincere. Judy felt her joy would burst out.

She watched his lips move so slightly when he mouthed the phrases Pastor Tyson spoke first. She smiled when he handed the rings to the pastor with a steady hand.

"I now pronounce you husband and wife!"

Judy broke eye contact with Hart long enough to clap with abandon as Bryce and Ardyth Edwards shared their first wedded embrace. She held tight to Hart's arm as he led her down the aisle after the newlyweds.

Judy lost herself in more family heirlooms from Una's wonderful trunk. She sat in the attic, wrapped in a heavy woolen blanket, caressing Louise's baby shoes and a lock of her hair. Una's family's immigration papers. A pair of woolen slippers and a carved wooden pipe.

"Judy! Don't tell me you're up there again."

"All right, I won't," Judy called to Hart.

She heard him clomp up the steps. "What's so fascinating now? We've got the Porters all set up in the spare room. Aha." Hart plopped beside her, giving her cold nose a kiss.

"We never finished going through Aunt Una's trunk."

Hart picked up the fragile wedding veil. "I think you'll make a gorgeous bride in this."

"As gorgeous as Ardyth?"

"At least." He set the brittle lace gently on her head.

Hart took Judy's hands in his and captured her gaze. Without moving his eyes from hers, Hart reached into his pocket and slipped a warm metal circle covered with sparkly diamonds onto her finger. "I took a page out of Bryce's book and had this engraved. But I didn't take any chances with a letter. Will you marry me?"

"Awfully sure of yourself, aren't you?"

Hart cupped Judy's face. "Sure of us," he said, sealing his promise with a kiss.

Lisa Lickel lives in southern Wisconsin with her husband, a high school science teacher. Lisa performs and writes radio dramas, reads every spare minute, loves to travel, quilts, and putters in the flower garden. She is involved in every historical society within driving distance, a tribute to her BS degree in History and Russian studies.

You may correspond with this author by writing:
Lisa J. Lickel
Author Relations
PO Box 721
Uhrichsville, OH 44683

A Letter to Our Readers

Dear Reader:

In order to help us satisfy your quest for more great mystery stories, we would appreciate it if you would take a few minutes to respond to the following questions. We welcome your comments and read each form and letter we receive. When completed, please return to:

Fiction Editor
Heartsong Presents—MYSTERIES!
PO Box 721
Uhrichsville, Ohio 44683

Did you enjoy reading *The Gold Standard* by Lisa J. Lickel?

Very much! I would like to see more books like this! The one thing I particularly enjoyed about this story was:

_____
_____
_____

Moderately. I would have enjoyed it more if:

_____
_____
_____

Are you a member of the HP—MYSTERIES! Book Club?
Yes   No

If no, where did you purchase this book?

_____

Please rate the following elements using a scale of 1 (poor) to 10 (superior):

___ Main character/sleuth   ___ Romance elements

___ Inspirational theme   ___ Secondary characters

___ Setting   ___ Mystery plot

How would you rate the cover design on a scale of 1 (poor) to 5 (superior)? _____

What themes/settings would you like to see in future **Heartsong Presents—MYSTERIES!** selections? _____

_____

_____

_____

Please check your age range:

- ◯ Under 18
- ◯ 18–24
- ◯ 25–34
- ◯ 35–45
- ◯ 46–55
- ◯ Over 55

Name: _____

Occupation: _____

Address: _____

E-mail address: _____